P9-DHG-784
WITHDRAWN

A Kind of Dream

Also by Kelly Cherry

Fiction

The Woman Who
We Can Still Be Friends
The Society of Friends
My Life and Dr. Joyce Brothers
The Lost Traveller's Dream
In the Wink of an Eye
Augusta Played
Sick and Full of Burning

Poetry

The Life and Death of Poetry
The Retreats of Thought
Hazard and Prospect: New and Selected Poems
Rising Venus
Death and Transfiguration
God's Loud Hand
Natural Theology
Relativity: A Point of View
Lovers and Agnostics

Nonfiction

Girl in a Library: On Women Writers and the Writing Life
History, Passion, Freedom, Death and Hope: Prose about Poetry
Writing the World
The Exiled Heart: A Meditative Autobiography

Chapbooks/Limited Editions

Vectors: J. Robert Oppenheimer: The Years before the Bomb, poems
The Globe and the Brain, an essay
Welsh Table Talk, poems
An Other Woman, a poem
The Poem, an essay
Time out of Mind, poems
Benjamin John, a poem
Songs for a Soviet Composer, poems
Conversion, a story

Translation

Antigone, in *Sophocles,* ed. David R. Slavitt and Palmer Bovie, vol. 2
Octavia, in *Seneca: The Tragedies,* ed. David R. Slavitt, vol. 2

A Kind of Dream

Stories

Kelly Cherry

Terrace Books
A trade imprint of the University of Wisconsin Press

Terrace Books, a trade imprint of the University of Wisconsin Press, takes its name from the Memorial Union Terrace, located at the University of Wisconsin–Madison. Since its inception in 1907, the Wisconsin Union has provided a venue for students, faculty, staff, and alumni to debate art, music, politics, and the issues of the day. It is a place where theater, music, drama, literature, dance, outdoor activities, and major speakers are made available to the campus and the community. To learn more about the Union, visit www.union.wisc.edu.

Terrace Books
A trade imprint of the University of Wisconsin Press
1930 Monroe Street, 3rd Floor
Madison, Wisconsin 53711-2059
uwpress.wisc.edu

3 Henrietta Street
London WC2E 8LU, England
eurospanbookstore.com

Printed in the United States of America

Library of Congress Cataloging-in-Publication Data

Cherry, Kelly, author.
[Short stories. Selections]
A kind of dream: stories / Kelly Cherry.
pages cm
ISBN 978-0-299-29760-2 (cloth: alk. paper)
ISBN 978-0-299-29763-3 (e-book)
I. Title.
PS3553.H357A6 2014
813′.54—dc23
2013037616

To

BURKE

O! for a muse of fire, that would ascend the brightest heaven of invention.

Prologue, *Henry V*,
William Shakespeare

All knowledge, the totality of all questions and all answers is contained in the dog.

"Investigations of a Dog,"
Franz Kafka

. . . the eternal Light . . .
Within its depths I saw gathered together,
Bound by love into a single volume,
Leaves that lie scattered through the universe.

Paradiso XXXIII, 85–87, *The Divine Comedy*,
Dante Alighieri, tr. James Finn Cotter

Contents

Acknowledgments

"On Familiar Terms" first appeared in *blackbird* (www.vcu.edu/blackbird) and was the inaugural winner of the Rebecca Mitchell Tarumoto Short Fiction Prize for best story in the magazine in 2011. "Story Hour" first appeared in *Commentary*. "On the Care and Handling of Infants and Small Children" first appeared in *The Iron Horse Review*. "All the Little Dogs" first appeared in a special issue of *The Seattle Review*, edited by David Shields. "Faith, Hope, and Clarity" first appeared in *The Western Humanities Review*.

The author is deeply grateful to the Virginia Center for the Creative Arts for residencies during which these stories were drafted or revised.

A Kind of Dream

Prologue: On Familiar Terms

Forebears

n., descriptive, usually with direct objects. At the turn of the twentieth century, Hattie Little married a quiet, polite, hard-working Yankee who'd come south to find work, which he did, as a sawyer for a lumber mill, and also found her, a small woman with waist-length auburn hair, a spotless record of attendance at the Presbyterian Church, and a love of dancing parties. They married and had three daughters (and two stillborn sons whose headstones were in the backyard). The first daughter became a librarian and married a man with orange groves in Florida. The second was a bit of a flapper, flirtatious and partial to the Charleston, and she eloped. The youngest, Eleanor, asked for violin lessons. She had learned to read music by copying the notes from her eldest sister's piano étude books. Eleanor's father, the Yankee sawyer and a fine carpenter, gave her an old fiddle that had belonged to his father. It was enough to learn on, but the sound was terrible. The New Orleans *Times-Picayune* ran a weekly essay contest; she won it weekly until she had fifty dollars and could order from the Montgomery Ward catalogue a new violin, with case, bow, and a cake of real rosin. The sound wasn't altogether terrible but it was fairly awful. Until then, she had scraped sap, dry and hardened, from pine bark. Her father was himself a serious aficionado of classical music, and because of that was considered a little strange, but Hattie was so well liked that the neighbors put up with the music. This was in Louisiana—bayou country—and then Mississippi.

In South Carolina, a lawyer who loved Shakespeare, frequently rereading the plays in his office when he was supposed to be working, married a woman seventeen years younger than he. She was slender and dark-haired, with piercing eyes; he was redheaded, going gray, and eventually went white. She taught drama and mathematics. She was herself dramatic and told outrageous stories. She would have been a princess, she said, if an ancestor had not thrown away her crown to marry a Portuguese commoner. She told her children they were descended from John Marshall, signer of the Declaration of Independence. Huguenot ancestors had fled from Switzerland to Ireland. She began to believe her stories. The lawyer and the drama teacher had two boys and two girls. (The younger girl, discovering that their cat had had a litter of kittens in the rain, brought the kittens indoors and tried to dry them out by putting them in the oven. She turned it on so they wouldn't catch a chill.) The town held the lawyer in high esteem—"Judge," they called him—but he would work only for the defense and, sadly, Rock Hill had few people who needed defending. When his chief client—his brother (!)—died, the Judge went broke. Very broke. As broke as a rusted bike with no wheels, no basket, and no seat. No handles, either. Their youngest child, a boy, heard a violin being played, was ravished by the sound of it, and made one from a cigar box following directions from *The Book of Knowledge*. He'd thought a violin made the most beautiful sound he ever heard, but the violin he'd made for himself did not, quite. The sound was so disappointing that he immediately constructed another violin, this time from bark, using a penknife to carve the f-holes. He got a job as a paperboy and saved his money until he could order an even better violin from Sears, Roebuck; it came with a cardboard case, a cake of rosin, and a copy of the National Tutor, a home-study method.

syn. Golden oldies.

Art and Eleanor

Compound subj. As people do, Art and Eleanor began as individuals. Art was the youngest in a genteel family fallen on hard times in South Carolina. Eleanor grew up in a bayou in Louisiana, where white egrets were a dime a dozen. Separately each discovered the violin in childhood and never doubted what they wanted to do, and when, having met, they realized they could do it together, they married and started a string quartet. They had to go outside the family to find the cellist and violist.

In the beginning, they were very much alike—naïve and passionate—but time charged them with a consciousness of particular tasks. Nearly mute with shyness, Ellie learned to dicker with tradespeople. She checked and doublechecked the household account. To save money, she rolled her own cigarettes with a little tin gadget. She urged Arthur to ask for a raise. (Teaching violin and theory did not pay well.) She went to work herself. Her boss chased her around the desk but she managed to keep him at arm's-length. She started an insurance agency and then she and Arthur each had two full-time jobs, plus the string quartet. Plus: Art taught summer school, accepted a year-round job as music director for a Methodist church, and established the Commonwealth Symphony. Plus: Eleanor developed a method for removing wallpaper and tried to market it, but someone stole the idea. Plus: this, that, and the other. When could they parent? There was no time for parenting. The kids were smart: Ellie and Art let them parent themselves. Perhaps the kids were not quite smart enough to avoid borrowing strangers' cars, reading during arithmetic, and getting bashed in the forehead with a baseball bat. Eleanor worked late at her day job. Arthur believed she was having an affair and pounded on the door to her office and yes, there was a man. A warm summer night. All the other offices dark. Art is quaking with rage, his voice louder than he himself has ever heard it. Are they having an affair? She says no, they are not having an affair, but the man says nothing, which Art takes to mean that they are having an affair. A fistfight is proposed, but Art is, after all, a violinist. His hands are important to him. Although she insists there is no affair, Ellie is annoyed that Art is unwilling to fight for her. The man, the man, the man—a corporal!—well, he walks out of the office and drives home, which leaves Art and Ellie facing each other under a buzzing fluorescent light tube. Where are their children? On Blueberry Hill? At a movie? A soda shop? Reading in their rooms? Hanging out with lowlifes? As the aunt who cooked the kittens said, "When parents love each other more than they love their children, everybody suffers."

Ellie perhaps has always wanted Arthur to be more like her father, but for that to happen she would have to be more like a daughter, and she can't be a daughter when she has to be a mother. Except that she can't be a mother because she has to work all the time. Maybe she likes working, but that doesn't make work *not* a *necessity*.

Arthur has a slightly different view; he thinks she needs him to keep her—in fact, the family—on an even keel. It is true that they seem to be always just one crisis away from catastrophe.

Several members of the nuclear family have on different occasions had the same thought: that *someone* among them loves drama. Loves the *Sturm und Drang* of it. But who could that be? There is nothing they would like better, they say—individually and collectively—than to live in peace and quiet. Before assuming that they are all guilty, we must remember that each has made strenuous efforts to escape the noise and confusion.

The Watchful Child

n. phr. The one who notices when Mother is angry, Father is hurt, Brother feels trapped, and Sis is scared. Or perhaps there is no Brother, no Sis, and the child must be a marriage counselor. Or perhaps Father has died, and the child becomes Mother's friend. Or Mother has deserted the family, run off with the manager of a chain of sporting goods stores in another state, and the child tries to take her place, packs a school lunch for Sis, polishes Brother's shoes at night as if the family lived in a hotel and not a house. Father lingers late at work, so the child helps Sis with her homework. Mother leaves her lover and returns on a train; she won't say why she left him. Brother is angry with her. Mother fights with Brother—voices in the dining room, urgent, heated whispers, things said that seem incomplete, referential, so that the child will spend a lifetime puzzling them out—and when Mother flees into her bedroom and slams the door, the child listens to Brother's story of how it was, their fighting, how it has been for as long as he can remember. The child can see the tears he does not shed. The child knows the Mother is a bright beautiful spirit eclipsed by circumstance. That Father is tender-hearted and wants more than anything for Mother to love him. The watchful child is the one who anticipates crisis and calamity, flinching when the telephone rings. The watchful child keeps a weather eye out, registering minute shifts in temperature and pressure. The watchful child has made plans to escape but worries that to leave the past behind is to betray it. The watchful child is afraid to blink, lest everyone disappear.

Everyone. For starters, there is no Sis; there is no manager of a chain of sporting goods stores.

See also giving; caring; panic attacks; would rather be heard than seen.

(*ex.* "The watchful child, awake in the dark, glances at the Mickey Mouse clock on the nightstand. Mickey's yellow-gloved hands point to ten and two."—Unknown. *ex.* "The watchful child observes the flowering snow."—Anon.)

syn. The child who writes everything down, to keep it safe. To keep it. The child who is afraid of being abandoned.

ant. A child who has been made welcome. The child who feels worthy enough to justify the parents' appalling sacrifices, the constant hardship of their lives. Their lack of freedom. The necessary forfeit of their closeness—those fall weekends watching football with a shared blanket over their laps, those mornings when they slept late on the screened porch, laughing, trying not to give themselves away to the milkman settling his bottles on the stoop.

Firstborn

n., adj. The son. He holds two opposing ideas about himself: that he is a genius and that he is a stupid person merely posing as a genius. The tests tell him one thing, and his fear of exposure tells him the other.

Other people's expectations burden him, especially his parents', but also his teachers'. He stops practicing the piano, because if he sticks with it he will have to become a great pianist, and he is not positive he has it in him to become a great pianist. He likes to draw and paint, but is he Michelangelo? Probably not. He likes acting, but really, how manly can an actor be, playing make-believe? He decides to become a writer.

But first he wants to get in Susan Herring's pants, and since her father is a Baptist preacher, he offers to take a turn at the pulpit to get in his good graces. He delivers an impassioned sermon on Daniel in the lions' den. Mrs. Herring invites him to Sunday dinner. He and Susan do it in the church cloakroom.

He and Susan do it on one of the pews.

He and Susan do it in the choir loft.

He tells his parents that he is in love and wants to marry Susan. He is seventeen, Susan sixteen. His parents tell her parents. It is 1950. Susan goes to Baltimore to live with her grandparents for the rest of the year. He finishes high school but arrives late for graduation because the transmission falls out of his jalopy and he has to run the last three miles.

His parents were there, for once.

The gifted child, when surrounded by other gifted children, may become nervous. There is a risk of no longer being the most gifted child in the room. He has already been drinking for a year or two to ease his anxiety, to smooth out the bumps, to stay cool. He likes to be in charge and most of the time is. He breezes through the draft board's I.Q. test, deliberately scoring low, then, when the so-called monitor nods off, other students slip him their tests. He fills in the correct answers for half a dozen rural kids eager to go to Korea. Let's hope they didn't find themselves on Pork Chop Hill. He drops out of college, marries (not Susan), marries again (still not Susan), marries a third time (no, not Susan, never Susan), and finally stops marrying and just lives with women. He drinks from the time he gets up until he passes out for the night, but even so he writes a memoir and becomes briefly famous. A few years later he is getting rolled in a ditch on his way home from the liquor store, his fine watch gone forever. His daughter has a tough row to hoe.

But why in God's name should anybody begrudge him a drink? He has always shouldered the responsibility for so much. Everyone depends on him, and he has only so much to give. It's like he has to carry the whole fuckass world on his shoulders. Even when he was a kid, he was always being called away from his friends and made to babysit his kid sister. Why couldn't his parents stay home and do their own babysitting? Why does he always have to look after everybody, smooth things out, make things right, cheer the family up, kiss his sister on the cheek after she and her husband are pronounced man and wife (his father was too dazed and confused to understand that he was supposed to do that), teach his father to be a man, his mother how to be human?

Before he dies—early, of alcoholism—he takes to telling people that the only thing an I.Q. test tells you is how well you can take an I.Q. test.

syn. The son. The one who carries the cross.

ant. A free man. A man who has succeeded in disentangling himself from himself.

The Son's Daughter

Née Babette Bryant. *A/k/a* BB.

syn. Nina's niece; mother of Nina's adopted daughter.

syn. Art and Ellie's granddaughter; partner of Roy.

etym. Babette Bryant lives with her mother in Georgia and longs for her dad, seeing him only on holidays. She is a peach-colored baby with gray eyes that turn green as she metamorphoses into a little girl. By the time she is three, she is a stunner, with long chestnut hair, dark, skeptical eyebrows, and high cheekbones. People tell her how beautiful she is, but she doesn't feel beautiful; she thinks they are trying to make her feel better about being hard of hearing. She wears a hearing aid. At twelve, she and her mother, Janice, fight about things like when she can date, her homework, the way she dresses (tight, hip-hugging jeans and tops that barely cover her nascent breasts). She's allowed a delicate, discreet tattoo on her ankle but Janice nixes the belly ring. She bumps into a guy while wearing headphones and, not telling her mother, goes out with Roy Dante, an older man (twenty-two) who hangs out at the pool hall and in beer joints but does not, as it happens, shoot up or snort anything, which is surprising, because he deals drugs. He won't let her use. He wants to make movies. He doesn't know how he's going to do this but he thinks about it all the time; he dreams up plots and figures out the camera angles. He tells her he will put her in his movies. She will be a star, her name in lights. She absorbs every word he says as if it is a kind of drug. She loses her virginity to him and wham-O, she's knocked up. She's thirteen. Babette hitches from Georgia to Connecticut to see her dad and tell him that she's pregnant, but the woman he's living with—it's her house—won't allow her to stay. Her father, Nina's brother, ships her to Madison, Wisconsin, via bus, without informing Nina of the pregnancy. Babette is now fourteen, "going on fifteen," as she explains. Her aunt Nina will look after her until the baby is due. Roy visits her while she is there and they have sex again and talk about running off to Hollywood, but first she goes home to have the baby. She doesn't even name it, refuses to see it, does not want to believe it is real. At Babette's dad's funeral, her mother gives the baby to her aunt, who will adopt her ("it" is a girl). While her mother is in Connecticut doing this, she and Roy take off for Hollywood, hitching most of the way. They have no money. Because of her, Roy has quit dealing. She says she can earn money for them. He is baffled until he looks her in the eye. "Forget it," he says, in a voice that kind of scares her. "You are not going to turn tricks." He gets a job in a studio mailroom, realizes there is no future in it, gets another job as a lowly assistant in an agent's office, begins to make money and takes classes for a high school equivalency degree.

She makes a stab at acting lessons, decides she'll never be a real actress but discovers that the camera adores her even without talent. She is one of the rare lucky ones. Roy meets people, makes connections, enrolls in film school. His minimal education is no hindrance in Hollywood. He has directed BB in every movie she's made. He understands everything about her: the vagaries of her mind, what she can and cannot portray, the way morning light cups her profile and evening light exaggerates her eyes, the angles from which she looks her best. At his urging, she goes professionally by her initials: BB. On posters, on marquees: BB.

Still in her thirties, she finds herself with child again. Her skin glows. She smiles a lot, even when she's by herself. She and Roy tell their two best friends, Lola and Terry, but swear them to silence. Not even one paparazzo gets wind of it.

The baby girl is born prematurely. She is so miniscule that the hospital won't let them hold her. They stand at her cradle side by side, feeling the warmth of the heat lamp on their arms. They sing to her:

lullabies, Beatles, Johnny Cash, Janis Joplin. They hold hands and try prayer. The baby seems to be making progress, then her heart stops. Doctors, nurses, crash carts pile into the room, reducing the parents to spectators. The noise, the crowd, the hectic dance of medical personnel frighten them. Their baby's heart stays stopped. Now the hospital lets them hold their daughter, their very small, dead daughter. BB looks at Roy and says, over her daughter's body, each word carefully carved and placed, "If you're going to leave me someday because of this, do it now. If you try to do it later, I'll kill you." The look in her eyes is hard, reckless, and so unforgiving that he believes she would do it, but he knows he will never want to be with anyone but her.

He has directed a few well-received movies, and now he finds the backing to make what he thinks of as "the big one." He is charming and competent, well dressed in cashmere, silk, denim, and leather, wears a gold bracelet, and has an easy but forceful way with actors. It is his script he will be directing this time. The movie is set in Afghanistan, and they shoot in Mongolia. (The war in Afghanistan is in what can only be called its umpteenth year. The sky in Mongolia is broad and blue, and at night the moon so big it seems to be next door.) It's a complicated film, with a cast only a little short of thousands, the logistics nerve-wracking. No digital backgrounds.

But yaks. Lots of yaks. Not in the movie. In Mongolia.

They are already famous enough, especially she—although she can't bear to watch herself on screen and never looks at her rushes—to have an entourage of publicists and bodyguards. Sets are constructed, props flown in or purchased locally; the cameras roll. As the female lead, she has been made up to look as if she has just returned from a skirmish, with scratches on her high cheekbones and fake blood on her forehead, her camouflage shirt partly unbuttoned, the pants coming untucked from heavy black boots. She enters the cave, lays down her Kalashnikov rifle, and says, "We're fucked." She does this over and over again, the same two words, until Roy feels he has everything right—the angle, the light, her face, her inflection, every infinitesimal movement, the composition of the whole. When they wrap the scene, the bodyguards are playing poker outside the set. He joins them, expecting BB to hang around and watch them for at least a little while, but she has her driver take her back to the hotel.

Ulan Bator (also known as Ulaanbaatar) is cold, with winds that seem to swoop down the streets like Chinggis Khaan and his terrifying, conquering tribe. In the hotel bar, a throat-singer produces unearthly sounds, as if echoing a cry from a distant planet. BB turns her hearing aid off and orders a cognac. She has begun to think about their first baby, the one she gave away, the other girl. How is she? How is she doing in school? She would now be older than BB was when she gave birth to her.

What color are her eyes? Did they darken as she grew? What does she like to eat? What is her favorite song? (Though knowing Aunt Nina, she probably hears only classical music.) Her favorite color, favorite flavor of ice cream?

Her child wouldn't remember her, but maybe her child's flesh remembers her. Maybe she can sense that BB is thinking about her. Probably she doesn't put it in words to herself, but maybe her body remembers having been in BB's body. It's not necessarily a crazy thought. New studies show that babies in utero are far more aware than anyone ever suspected.

The cognac makes her feel warm inside but in her room—they have a suite—the cold lurks behind the drapes, weasels its way bedward. She puts on silk pajamas and slides under the covers. She thinks she can still hear the throat-singer, but that's impossible. Her hearing aid is in a case on the counter next to the sink in the bathroom.

The hotel is next to the Gorki-Terelj National Park. She knows she will wake to a view of a meadow dotted with edelweiss and a mountain toothpicked with pines. The furniture is antique, the floors are marble, there is local art on all the walls, some of it involving expensive fabric (silk, cashmere, camel hair). She has made use of the indoor pool, the fitness center, and the Asian spa, but tonight none of this interests her.

It's too early to go to sleep, so she thinks some more about her first child. These are the first thoughts she has allowed herself to think about her first child in twenty-five years.

Not that she never caught herself thinking *underneath* her conscious thoughts. Brief images, glimpses, flashes, but she always shoved them back under, below the level of sentences. She never even stayed in touch with Aunt Nina.

She lies in the dark, thinking.

A few days later she decides to call her aunt in Wisconsin when she and Roy get back to the States.

Maybe she'll tell Roy and maybe she won't.

Tavy

abbr. Octavia.

pronounced Tā•vee.

vb. Emphatically a verb. Tavy, Nina's adoptee and BB's first child, green-eyed and stubborn, broke upon the earth like a tsunami. She was feisty, independent, demanding, impatient. Perhaps she bore certain qualities inherited from her great-grandmother Eleanor. From the beginning, Tavy's interior life was a tumult. Emotions knocked her this way and that. But even as a child she knew what she wanted to do: In elementary school she learned, with the rest of her class, to make pictures with crayons, pastel chalks, and finger paints, but she made more pictures, used up more chalk, more finger paint than anybody else. In the fifth and sixth grades she worked with construction paper and collage, and she approached her projects with an odd seriousness, as if she were already thinking of their place in the record of her life, though of course she wasn't. She was simply intense by nature.

And though she didn't know it, her mother knew that Tavy was more focused than her grandfather, who had drawn and painted but was distracted by writing, theater, philosophy, mathematics, anthropology, chess, poker, Go, bars, women, and talk.

In her mother's house books were everywhere, on shelves, stacked on the floor, in the kitchen, in the bedrooms, and Tavy loved to read. She had her own library card and checked books out every week, taking them back the next week. She held opinions about what she read and regularly delivered book reviews to her mother and father. Vocally. "This book is good. It doesn't make me wish I were doing something else while I'm reading it," she said.

In a book at home Tavy saw a photograph of an object made by Joseph Cornell. She decided she would make one for herself. She began collecting objects—a blue pebble, a small pocketbook mirror, some blue scylla from the yard, two hickory nuts, a maple key, the stub of a pencil, a nail, a paperclip from her mother's desk, a square of gold wrapping paper that she cut into a star, and a dead cricket. She showed the concoction to her mother. Nina studied it, especially the dead cricket, wondering if she should explain carnal decomposition to her daughter. It seemed much too soon.

Nina's daughter the assemblage artist.

Her mother began bringing art books home from the university's art library. Nina's husband, who had legally adopted Tavy when she was five, took her to his office in the History Department and let her flip through his books on Romanesque, Medieval, and Renaissance art.

She took up body painting. One day, when she was six, she entered her mother's study with a blue nose. Nina made a joke about people with blue noses. Tavy didn't get the joke, but she took the attention as approval.

Her stepfather gave her a flat tin of watercolors and brushes, and she filled the paper with bare, brown trees. She explained to her mother that she didn't have to paint the snow, because the snow was the paper itself. What was in the rectangle was snow.

When she made a picture, she felt as if she were flying. As if she were soaring above the world but also as if she had magic eyes that let her see the smallest detail on the ground.

After she started using charcoal and oil paints, Tavy always had smudges of one or the other on her face and hands.

Tavy did not recall a time when she had not loved her stepfather, but sometimes she wondered where her "real" father was. "Daddy is your real father," her mother told her. "He's the one who is flesh and blood and here, and he loves you."

"Okay," Tavy said, "where is the unreal one?" Her mother didn't know.

Tavy did not ask her mother, who had adopted her even before her stepfather did, where her real mother was. She didn't want to know. It would be too confusing, and anyway, she had decided that her real mother hated her. Why else would she give her away? Nina always told her that her birth mother loved her very, very much but couldn't take care of her, but as Tavy grew older she found this more difficult to believe. Why didn't her birth mother write? Why didn't she call?

When Tavy was little, Nina had a tendency to excuse Tavy's temper tantrums and contrariness as "high spirits," but after Nina married Palmer, he laid down some rules. When Tavy lost her temper, she had to apologize. If she used a bad word, she wasn't allowed to play with her art materials until she apologized. She became better about obeying rules, but she still broke them when she could get away with it.

At an early age, Tavy had encountered death three times. She had seen her great-grandmother die in England; she had seen her dog die, sort of—she wasn't present for his death, but she had seen him old and sick and knew he was dying; and her favorite teacher, Miss Lathrop, was murdered in the public library right in front of her. She still thought about it sometimes, the man with the gun, the man who tried to protect Miss Lathrop, and Miss Lathrop, her wonderful bookish friend with a gentle demeanor and soft voice. She assumed Miss Lathrop was in heaven, but she couldn't understand why God had taken her there. She thought it was selfish of him to take Miss Lathrop so far away that she couldn't even come to the library anymore.

In high school she went out with boys several times and necked with them and once went to third base but she didn't have sex even though plenty of girls she knew did. In college, at Evergreen, in Washington State, she had sex with the same boyfriend for two years. They drove through the snow-capped mountains, too many of them strip-mined, and stopped by rivers where salmon swam and spawned. The countryside was full of mule deer and bear, and once upon a time pronghorn roamed. (The Yakima Nation have reintroduced pronghorn to their land.) She and her boyfriend said tearful goodbyes on the last class day of his senior year, but neither expected or wanted the relationship to continue. He went off to be an intern in public service for the summer. She transferred to the university back home, where she graduated and started her M.F.A. Her parents let her stay home to paint. There were galleries in Madison, and more in Chicago. She gave notice that she would move out when she had saved a small nest egg. She was twenty.

In Madison, she hooked up with Zayed Mbawe. His parents had emigrated from West Africa, but he was pure America. He wore do-rags on his head, and jeans and a tee-shirt and a hoodie, an intricately wrought silver necklace, and an earring in each ear. He taught her about jazz, rap, hip hop, and rhythm and blues, all of which she knew would cause her mother to despair. She couldn't get enough of him, was addicted to him, would climb on him when he stretched out on the couch, would waylay him when he did laundry, sent him cell phone photos of her almost-naked self. Sex with him drugged her, made her dopey, made her want to run her tongue over every part of his body, made her think of him while she was painting, made her think of him while she was reading, made her kiss his eyelids, his ear-ringed ears, his curly hair, his sculpted face, his lean, hard, young body, his smooth hands, and the awesome architecture of his feet.

"My feet?" he asked, laughing at her. "You like my *feet*?" He stared down at his feet. "I guess they're all right, but—"

Sex was a haze, a daze, a maze. All day her skin remembered his. Everywhere she went she felt surrounded by a sexual force field.

But he had a wandering eye, and she caught him looking at Jewel, and then Ondine, a girl she had known since kindergarten. A week later, someone told her Zayed had been spotted at a party with Coco Untermeyer. In her room at night, Tavy sobbed until her eyes were dry and her throat sore, but everywhere she went she stood tall and erect and acted as if nothing bothered her.

Why wasn't she on the Pill? They used condoms, she had insisted on that, but maybe he'd been too slow putting it on or the condom broke. Two months passed without her period. She thought about having an abortion; that was the sensible thing to do. But she also thought about how Nina had waited too long to have a child and had been unable to conceive. Maybe it would be better to have a child now, while she was young. She could continue to live at home a while longer and nothing on earth would stop her from making art.

Through all of this, Nina ached on her behalf. She saw how her daughter was whipsawed by emotion and wished she could convince her that things would get better when she was older but the words were meaningless to a young girl in the throes, the thrall, of love. A girl who did not yet understand how long a life could be. (Or how short.)

Nina explained to Palmer that their daughter would be living with them for a while longer. And that a new infant would be joining their household.

Palmer

Proper n.

Semi-proper man.

In her forties Nina married Palmer Wright, who taught medieval history at the university, a place of such specialized specialization that scholars did not have areas or fields or subjects or texts so much as they had page numbers. Professor X did his work on p. 119 while Professor Y did hers on p. 194. This had got to Palmer, as had the loneliness and boredom he experienced in the wake of his divorce. He wanted to expand his imagination, to think about English in a new way. He was no weak-chinned Casaubon. What he needed in his life, he felt, was a creative writer, and as it happened they were not hard to find, inasmuch as they could be found on the sixth floor.

He sympathized with Tavy's struggle to define herself. It would be hard, he thought, to have a great-aunt for a mother, a writer for a mother, and no grandparents. When Nina was working, he took Tavy for walks, helped her with homework, commented on the pictures she made and brought to him, and became well acquainted with the school principal, since the child was always causing trouble. He tried to maintain a stern mien when he collected her from the principal's office, but in his heart he was rooting for her.

When he learned that Tavy was pregnant, his first thought was how great it would be to be a grandfather. His second was to find the guy and beat him up or at least make him marry Tavy. When Tavy said she didn't want to marry Zayed, his first thought returned. When Tavy had morning sickness, he stood behind her and held her hair back from her face as she leaned over the toilet.

Strenuous Efforts at Escape

In some houses there are trapdoors. They turn up anywhere, everywhere. You are standing in the middle of a room, not worried about anything, just standing and looking around, and the floor gives way and you drop down. Now you're under the house. It's possible, even probable, that other family members are also under the house, but they are never on the same level you are on. So you are alone where you are, there, under the house. And the floor above is never high enough for you to stand up without crouching. So you have to bend over and semi-crawl your way out. Yes, you live in a crawl space. You'd suppose you might run into someone sometimes but that never happens—not in a house of secrets. You crawl your way out, which takes an hour or a day or two or a month or a year, and then you reenter the house, and boom, another trapdoor opens and you have to go through the whole process again. Is this exhausting? It is exhausting. Do you want to escape? Of course you want to escape. It's very strange, the fact that the house is always there and you are always in it. But that's what houses with trapdoors are like.

Callie Wright

conj. Callie, named for the muse—and for an instrument her mother remembers distantly hearing as a little girl—has her grandmother Nina's preoccupied, soulful eyes but not her ivory skin. Callie's skin is light olive. Her hair is dark and curly, surrounding her face like a nimbus. Like her great-great-grandparents, the first time she hears a violin (the Six-State Calliope Convention no longer convenes in Madison) she insists on lessons. She has an instinct for it, as a dog has an instinct to bark or a bird to sing. Nina, who is also her great-aunt, buys her a sixteenth-size violin, which she treats as tenderly as another child might a beloved china doll. She learns to play "Come to Jesus" in whole notes. She listens to Nina and Palmer's and her mother's CDs.

A sixteenth! How can it include a bridge, f-holes, pegs, sounding post, string nuts? The whole thing is so tiny it looks like a toy. No, surely it is too delicate to be a toy. It looks like a piece of jewelry. It has been used, which gives it a warm sound. The ribs have been well seasoned. Soon Callie will play an eighth-, then a quarter-size violin.

How surprising that Callie, the daughter of a whirlwind, lives and moves in a patch of calm weather, as if insulated from tumult. Her mother has financial problems, artistic problems, boyfriend problems. Callie's straight, narrow nose turns up at her mother's antics. She loves her mother—and appreciates what her mother does for her—but even at five she seems to think fretting, crying, raging are time-wasters. Time, she was apparently born knowing, is both limited and valuable. How can she know this so early in her life? Or maybe she doesn't really know it, maybe she's simply gifted with inner peace the way she is naturally fitted for the violin? Maybe her serenity, her imperturbability stem from her having been born late in the scheme of things, after so much else has happened. From time to time she feels a bit sad, but when she is sad, she listens to music and then she is happy again. Even *sad* music makes her happy. At first she listens to ballet music, thrills to "Night on Bald Mountain," is elated by "The Moldau," and sings along with Carmen and Madama Butterfly, dropping down an octave when the music goes too high, but soon it is Mozart and nothing but Mozart, and then Bach, Bach, Bach, and when she arrives at the string quartets of Ludwig van Beethoven, which happens surprisingly fast, and long before she can play them, she feels she has found her true home, the one in which she can dwell undisturbed, as if on another planet, a green and gold planet from whose several silver moons issues a heavenly sound. Here she has the most intimate relationship of her life. She is one with the music. It moves her, it caresses, it enriches her. It makes her know things she cannot put into words.

Is it a dream, then, music? Does it separate you from people? It does, she thinks, and it doesn't. Through music, she knows people, their innermost feelings. Music is a real and reckonable force in the world. It speaks to everyone, knows everything—or rather, some music does. Beethoven's music does. She wants to be able to play the string quartets. And she wants to play *first* violin.

So her grandmother, who is also her great-grandmother, also her great-aunt and great-great-aunt, tells her about Art and Ellie, how they had their own string quartet and rehearsed in the living room and gave concerts. Nina tells her about Eleanor's evening gowns and the tenement apartment building, about how handsome Arthur looked in dress shirt, white tie, and tails, how the room was fogged with cigarette smoke when they were practicing (and when they were not practicing, too). How there were ashtrays on footstools between the stands. How Eleanor would have a bottle of Coke and a Hershey bar with almonds on her footstool, next to a pack of cigarettes, while Art always had a cup of coffee, with chicory and two spoonfuls of sugar, on his, until to save money he had to give up ordering chicory coffee from Louisiana. How they had such a good time practicing but Eleanor vomited before every concert. How they loved to play together.

Callie registers some of this and forgets some of it, but it helps her feel that what she aims to do has been validated in advance. She does not yet have the words to say this, but this is what she feels and it is what she will carry into adulthood.

Story Hour

When Larry's first wife left him, he wept a bit and went to bed but then he had to get back to work. Eventually he began to date, but he didn't like playing the field. For about a year he had an affair with an older woman who owned an art gallery. That came to an end and he married his secretary, Billie. When Billie left him, he went to bed and stayed there so long that finally the office called and said they were sorry and they hoped he would feel better soon but in the meantime were going to have to let him go. Billie got worried and started bringing him casseroles and carrot cake. "Don't misread this," she warned him. "I'd feel the same concern for any hurt creature I saw hugging the shoulder of a highway."

Larry did not get up. When your second ex-wife tells you she thinks of you as roadkill, you do not get up.

Larry did not get up until Aileen appeared on the scene. Billie had sent her over, Aileen said, to check on him. "She told me I should try to rouse you," she said.

Rouse or arouse?

"Who are you?" he asked, wondering if she was aware that when she leaned over to plump his pillow he could see down her tank-top.

"I'd do anything Billie asked me to do," Aileen said, which made Larry think he and Aileen had something in common. Her voice had a breathy quality, as if she'd just been running, or working out, or making love. "Billie's the best."

"How do you know her?" Larry asked.

"She's in my t'ai chi class." Aileen was looking around for a chair to pull up but Larry patted the mattress to indicate that she could sit on the bed beside him.

"T'ai chi. Is that like karate?"

"Silly," she said, smiling, and the soft liquidity of the syllables, the lovely uncomplication of her smile, the gentle sway of her breasts beneath Calvin Klein seemed to him like absolution. God or fate or somebody was forgiving him for being a fuckup, and after Aileen said goodbye, and after he had made her promise to stop in again tomorrow, he got up, showered, and shaved.

Aileen Lathrop thought about Larry the whole time she was cooking dinner for herself. He was thin. She bet that if she looked in his refrigerator she'd find all the food Billie said she had taken over there, and it would look like an experiment in biology by now.

When she had closed the dishwasher and started it running, she called Billie to report. "I think I'll look after him until he gets to feeling more up to things," she said. "I have time."

"It's not your job to be his nursemaid."

"I don't mind."

"Well," Billie said, "it would be a load off my mind. If you really don't mind."

"I don't," she said. "Really."

"Okay, then. Then it's okay."

"Okay."

Aileen put the cordless back in its charger. It was a warm evening, and from her apartment balcony she could watch the sun—which was as pink as a teenage girl's knees in June, as if the sun itself had been lying out in the sun all day and gotten sunburned—slowly leaving the sky. (In winter the Wisconsin sun was either a bright hard cough-drop yellow or the pale white of a convalescent Caucasian.)

A whisper of wind blew by, fluttering the pages of a leaflet she had absent-mindedly left out here. It fetched up against the rail.

The leaflet announced the month's library activities for children. Aileen worked at the public library. It was a job she loved. Children would hold out their books for her to stamp, and when she looked down into their faces she just knew the world was going to be saved.

Tavy was one of the kids who came to the library. Her mother dropped her off every Saturday morning and picked her up on the way back from the grocery store. By then, she had a stack of books in her arms so high it was always about to topple.

"Are you sure you want all these?" asked Miss Lathrop, the librarian, the pretty one who helped kids.

"I'm sure," Tavy said. There was nothing she hated more than running out of books in the middle of the week and not having anything to read until Saturday.

Miss Lathrop nodded. Miss Lathrop always asked Tavy this question, and Tavy always answered it the same way, and then Miss Lathrop always nodded. Tavy liked it when Miss Lathrop nodded. Miss Lathrop had curly red hair, and her curls bobbed when she nodded. If Tavy's mother ever died, she thought, she'd like Miss Lathrop as a substitute.

She thought about this as she sat on the slate ledge that fronted the library between the sidewalk and the negligible lawn and was higher next to the steps because the street sloped. But when her mother drove up, she forgot all about Miss Lathrop and jumped down, reaching back to grab a handful of books, running to put them in the front seat, running back to get the rest, and then getting into the car and pulling the door shut.

She had managed to get the whole stack of books from the library to the ledge in a single maneuver by clamping her chin on the top.

"Do you think you checked out enough to hold you till next Saturday?" her mother asked. Tavy liked the way her mother could smile with her voice.

"I couldn't help hearing the Story Hour story," Tavy said. Indeed, as she said this, it seemed to her that a spell had been placed on her and she had been unable to move away from the telling even though she had willed herself to, because Story Hour was for the little kids and Tavy was a big kid now.

"Is that so?" her mother said, knowing it was not only so but always so, and that that was why they had to get to the library every Saturday in time for Story Hour, even though neither of them ever mentioned that that was why.

Aileen told Larry about her job and how much she loved it and the children over swordfish steaks at The Blue Marlin. She wasn't sure if it was a date or not. If it was a date, it was wrong: she had no business going out with Billie's ex-husband. Yes, he was no longer married to Billie, but Billie was still Aileen's friend. But maybe it was not a date. Maybe she was only, like Billie, being friendly to Larry, helping him to get back on his feet. She reached for the butter, accidentally dragging her sleeve across the asparagus-with-Hollandaise-sauce on her plate.

"Here, let me get that," he said, gallantly, and moistened his napkin in his water glass and dabbed it at her sleeve.

"I'm afraid I'm always doing stuff like this. I'm a major klutz."

"Funny," he said, "you don't look like one."

She didn't dare ask him what he thought she looked like.

"You look like an angel," he volunteered. "An incredibly sexy angel."

She tried to pull her arm back but he was still dabbing. "I think it's fine now," she said.

"I don't want to let go of you," he said.

"I can't eat if you don't let go."

He let go but she wasn't ready and her arm dropped onto her plate. This time the Hollandaise was all over her sleeve. She burst into surprisingly loud tears.

"I'm sorry," he said. "It's my fault—"

She shook her head. "I told you, I'm a klutz."

"Don't cry," he said. "There's no use crying over spilled milk, or sleeves dipped in Hollandaise."

"That's not why I'm crying. I'm crying because I'm such a terrible person."

"I think I can safely say you are not a terrible person."

"How would you know?" she asked, gruffly. "Do you know anything about what goes on inside my head? Do you know I want to have sex with you?"

He gave this a moment's thought, then asked, "Would it be that awful to have sex with me?" He thought he might have stumbled onto the reason his wives kept leaving him. It was not going to be an easy reason to face up to, but it was better than knowing nothing.

He brightened when he remembered she had said she *wanted* to have sex with him. The breathiness in her voice had given that statement a curious little growl, and there was, he thought, something, if not quite tigerish, at least kittenish about her. Her reddish-blonde hair was fluffy, and her whole body seemed soft and boneless. He wanted to stroke her behind the ears.

Wherever.

"I never cheat on a girlfriend," she said.

"I'm sure Billie wouldn't think of it as cheating." Though, truthfully, he couldn't be sure of anything that Billie would think or not think. He certainly had not gotten it right when they were married.

"I will," she said, that odd bit of fierceness coming out again. "I'll think of it as cheating."

Since she was not using the subjunctive, he didn't argue. Better to quit while ahead. "You look like an angelic kitten," he said—but the words had come out backward. He felt so stupid that all he could do was stare at her. He had meant to say "kittenish angel."

She couldn't imagine what he meant, though she did find herself imagining a heaven where cute fluffy kittens with folded (since not currently in use) wings floated on cat-pillow clouds. The angel-kittens were purring angelically and yawning and napping. Could there be balls of yarn in heaven? She didn't see why the hell not, so she imagined the angel-kittens batting at balls of yarn, pulling the fuzzy threads loose with their claws, occasionally trying to unravel a tail and in general getting tangled up with the result that sometimes their wings were tied up every which way and, in short, the angel-kittens were grounded, if you could speak about a kitten, angel or otherwise, or indeed anything at all being grounded on a cloud, and she had to, imaginatively speaking, emancipate them from the rather dire situation they had gotten themselves into.

"Penny for your thoughts," he offered.

"Only a penny?" She let her gaze settle on him quietly, calmly, meeting his with a now-confident friendliness that she attributed to her recent success as a rescuer of cats. Aileen sometimes thought the best part of a day was the part you lived in your imagination. It was certainly one of the best parts. "I could get more, I'm sure." She smiled at him.

All week Tavy read the books she had checked out from the library. She pretended to be her favorite characters. "Ahoy!" she would call out when she got home from school, if she was pretending to be a pirate. She developed the most tragic cough when she read about Beth in *Little Women*. At the dinner table she reviewed the books for her parents, or for company, if they had company. She told their friend Sarah about *The Black Stallion*. She told Larry Adcock about *Rebecca of Sunnybrook Farm*. The summary of a single book could last to the last bite.

Sweeping and dusting and straightening up and especially putting clean sheets on the bed so it would look less like the sickbed of a patient suffering from terminal lethargy and not scare her off, he made up song titles to tell himself how he felt:

Larry's In Love
She's My Saucy Sweetheart
Larry's In Love And He'll Never Be Lonely Again (Except If She Has To Go Out Of Town To Visit A Sick Parent, Or Something)
I Got A Gal That's Got Looks And Books, Books And Looks
Nobody's Nicer'n Aileen
My Sweetheart Dragged Her Sleeve In The Hollandaise Sauce And Now She's My Saucy Sweetheart (the country-western version of *She's My Saucy Sweetheart*)

At t'ai chi Billie said, "How's Larry?"

"Oh," Aileen said, "he's better. He's getting out and about." Then she added, "We went to dinner."

"Oh?"

"What do you mean, 'Oh?'?"

Marie-Celeste did not like for her students to talk in class and she was now shooting dirty looks at Aileen and Billie that might have made Aileen squirm, except that Aileen was already squirming. "Are you dating Larry Adcock?" Billie asked.

"That's so funny," Aileen said, "that you'd call someone who used to be your husband by his whole name like that."

"It's not his whole name."

"It's not?" She shuddered a little, enough to make her almost lose her balance as she stood holding a pose on one leg. Was Larry not being honest with her? Was he keeping secrets?

"No, it's not."

Aileen put her other foot down, even though it wasn't time yet. She took a deep breath and exhaled before the guillotine fell. "Tell me his whole name," she said, resolutely.

"Larry Dickhead Adcock," Billie said, stretching. "That's his whole name. Larry Dickhead Adcock."

Aileen's heart filled with relief, a helium that would let her fly high. "Oh," she said, breathily, and feeling light and floating, and free, "oh my. Billie, you don't love him anymore!"

"I'm divorced from him, Aileen. For heaven's sake." Billie was wearing a black leotard with a low back and when she revolved on her mat Aileen could see the small tattoo between her shoulder blades. Aileen thought she would like to have a tattoo, too, but she wasn't big on pain. Billie completed her revolution and the teensy harp disappeared and Aileen found herself facing her friend again. "He wants children," Billie said.

"Didn't you?"

"I don't know," Billie said. "I just know I want to have fun first. I didn't take the age gap into enough consideration."

Marie-Celeste made a loud shushing noise designed not merely to warn the culprits but also to let everyone in the vicinity know that those being warned were indeed culprits and were making her life really unnecessarily hard. Aileen didn't pay any attention, since she made that noise several times a day herself, in the library.

"You don't really think he's a dickhead, though," she said.

"Sure I do. Why wouldn't I? Of course I do. It's not a pejorative term, particularly. Did you ever know a man who wasn't a dickhead?"

I thought t'ai chi would help me to be less of a klutz," Aileen told Larry as they were walking along the lakeside path to Picnic Point. "It's supposed to improve balance and general gracefulness."

"You're already better balanced than most women."

I Lean on Aileen.

"Do you mean you think most women are not as well balanced as men?"

"No, no," he answered, hurriedly. "I wouldn't say that."

"Because if that's what you think, it's no wonder you've been divorced twice."

He wanted to shoot himself. But, he thought, it looked as though the best he could do was to shoot himself in the foot. He was a man who could shoot himself in the foot while it was still in his mouth.

But he was also a man who had traded commodities. Who had driven a fork-lift at Menards during summers in college. Who had walked down the aisle twice and both times meant it when he promised to love and cherish. Why was he having so much trouble talking to a woman?

"I love you," he said.

She stopped walking and looked up at him. He saw her sunlit hair as a corona. "I love you too, Larry," she said.

"You do? Why?"

"I think you're very giving."

"I am," he said, surprised and happy to have discovered this. "I am very giving! I am a giving kind of guy!"

Since this was not something he had ever noticed before, he decided Aileen was brilliant. Brilliant, beautiful, and ballsy: what more could a man ask?

He had a dream that started out well, with people grinning and laughing, but something happened—something dark and blurred and rushed, like old home movies—and there was a birthday cake, outdoors, a cake on a table on a lawn, but a sudden summer storm blew the candles out, and then the cake was swimming in rain, was wet and crumbling, the little unlit pastel candles lying scattered on their sides in the grass. He woke staring into darkness and felt like he was staring at death: what it would be like; how it would be like nothing, the end of simile. For a few seconds, he couldn't tell which direction was up, which down, as if he had been cut loose from the earth's gravity and was yawing and pitching in space, where there *was* no up, no down, and he thought he might be about to be sick, but then the sensation slowed and stopped and he became aware of his head on the pillow, his body extended beneath the light coverlet, Aileen sleeping on her side with her back toward him, unsuspecting of any of what had just happened to him. He told himself to regularize his breathing. Was "regularize" a word? It was what he meant.

Poor Aileen. He didn't want her to know she'd gotten involved with someone who was half crazy.

A song called *Good Night, Aileen.*

The library had outgrown itself and computers, book carts, and personnel were crammed into every nook and cranny. Story Hour, which used to take place in its own room, had been squeezed out onto the open floor next to Checkout. The children sat in sturdy, small wood chairs painted primary colors. These were the little kids, of course; Tavy, who liked to say she had been reading books by herself for years now (she was six), wouldn't even think of joining them for Story Hour, but if she happened to be browsing through books on the nearby shelves while Miss Lathrop was reading aloud, could she help it if, given the excellent acoustics of a mostly unobstructed area, she overheard? If the story—about a funny little train that lacked self-confidence, or an elephant with ears as big as parachutes, or a princess who couldn't get a decent night's sleep because someone had stuck a pea under her mattress—if the story drifted all by itself across the lobby and entered her own (well-formed, close-to-her-head) ears, she certainly would not stop it, she was not going to slap her hands over her ears and shut the story out like a salesman or someone else who was importunate and rude, intrusive.

Aileen had always loved children and reading, so that she had never had any problem deciding what to do with her life. One of her teachers in college tried to get her to apply for graduate study in English. "You could be a scholar," the teacher had said, meaning, Aileen thought, like her. It had been an awkward moment, because she didn't want to hurt the teacher's feelings, but Aileen knew she couldn't be a scholar. Or maybe she could have been a scholar, but she could never have been a college teacher. She would have been terrified to walk into a seminar room full of students whose still relatively young faces had already hardened into attitude, whose minds were fortified by opinions barbative with transgression and theory, whose mouths clanged loudly with irony. She wanted to be liked, not rebutted. She wanted to be friends. When she sat at the front of the semicircle for Story Hour, the book open on her lap and the children, politely still or helplessly hyper, waiting for her to begin, she felt the warmth of them reaching her like light from the sun, or heat from a hearth.

Larry, on the other hand, needed a job. He went to the Job Fair. The applicants milled among long tables upon which application forms and company information sheets were stacked and behind which Human Resources, with a cheerful, expectant expression on his face, leaned back in a beige metal folding chair, feet up on the table, and showed a gap of hairy calf between sock and pantleg. The room was crowded, and Human Resources was multiple, like clones. "Are you interested in working with us?" asked Human Resources, carefully not saying *for*, as in *for us*.

Larry nodded.

"We anticipate several openings. What kind of position did you have in mind?"

"Your job looks good," Larry said, in a friendly way.

"Shit, yes," said a voice behind him. "Why don't we have cushy jobs like his?"

The guy behind, when Larry turned to look at him, had a drawn look. An overdrawn look, actually. He looked tired, hunted, perhaps by creditors calling him at home all hours of the day and night. "Lowest unemployment in the entire country except for Columbia, Missouri, do you believe it?"

Not wanting to antagonize him, Larry shook his head, but slowly.

Despite the tired look, the guy's conversation had seemed forced out of him, as if pressured by an internal engine about to combust. Larry could feel his carbonized breath on his face, something like a slap, no, nothing like a slap, and yet—yes, the slap of it, the spongy, deadly slap.

Larry took a step away, trying to gauge the right distance—enough to show separation; not so much as to give offense.

And it seemed that exactly the right distance had been established, because the guy stayed put.

Other voices carried from other tables, other applicants flipped through other folders.

Larry made a quarter-turn, getting ready to walk away, but Human Resources called after him, "What kind of experience do you have?"

The other guy didn't say anything but kept looking at Larry as if he, too, wanted to know the answer to this question.

Pieces of paper were strewn all over the floor. On the wall one of those institutional round clocks jumped every minute like the celebrated jumping frog of Calaveras County. The second hand spun noiselessly.

"I broker commodities," Larry said. "I mean, I used to."

Human Resources nodded knowingly. "Got burned out, I bet," said Human Resources. "It's a helluva demanding job."

"You weren't fired?" the drawn-looking guy said to Larry. "You weren't downsized?"

"I was let go when I stopped coming in," Larry said, defensively, feeling a need to prove that he was just as down and out as the next fellow.

"But you could go back to it." His eyes seemed to have come unmoored, as if they were at sea instead of seeing, the pupils dark and deep and drowning. His lips had turned in on themselves, constructing a dam against pressure. His left leg jittered, a dance of nerves, a sciatic tic. "Anytime you want, you could get back in and make a million bucks."

"I wouldn't say that," Larry said, thinking, *What a jerk*. "Not a million bucks."

"Not a million bucks," the guy said.

Larry got angry. "What's it to you? It's none of your business." To hell with the fucking nosy asshole. He addressed Human Resources: "I was thinking of moving into consulting. A financial counselor. I've got my broker's license already, and way more than the two years you need for the CFP."

Probably the words *financial counselor* were not what the guy wanted to hear right then. "I'm making it my business," he said. The jerk—the weirdo, the class-A bizzaro—slammed his fist down on the table, and the table bucked slightly, as if it were alive and had felt the blow. It was one of those aluminum tables with a brown top with a fake grain, held up by hollow aluminum legs, designed to be folded and stored alongside the beige metal folding chairs. "I fucking don't got no other. It's the only fucking business I have."

Larry and Human Resources held their breath. Without saying anything, even without looking at each other, Larry knew he and Human Resources were both registering, and registering that the other was registering, the swimming eyes, the jumping leg, the mouth like a Soviet hydro-electric plant, set as hard as concrete. Walloping a table might be the least of it. He didn't even let himself think what might be the most of it.

The by-now-quite-scary guy suddenly ripped himself away as if he were choking and needed air, and Larry said, "Hey, it's gotta get better from here, have a good one," and Human Resources said, "We get all kinds. They come in off the street, you know." Larry said, "I guess we all do. Come in off the streets," and this time when he turned to walk away Human Resources didn't call him back.

He had an uneasy feeling that the guy was following him but when he turned around and didn't see him he told himself to stop spooking himself. Men didn't stalk men, for God's sake.

What to do with himself, he wondered. Not so long ago he would have slept through the afternoon, but he could no longer nap his life away. He wished he could say Aileen's name—"Aileen"—and bingo, just like that she'd be here. Even if he had magical powers, he doubted she would leave work. She was too responsible for that. Plus, she loved her work. He went for a walk along Picnic Point by himself. He couldn't stop thinking about her.

He was *Addicted to Aileen*.

He had thought that there could not possibly be a third girl in the world who would ever be interested in marrying him, and that if, by some fluke, there was, he would not be interested in marrying her. What was the point in all the pain that would inevitably ensue? Some kinds of pain you could not avoid, everyone went through them, but there was no law that said you had to marry a woman, wait for her to dump you, and then spend months and months piecing together what you'd done, what she'd done, why it had gone wrong. That is what he had thought *before* he met Aileen.

Thinking about her, he forgot about the feeling of being followed.

Tavy leaned into the free-standing shelves, peering through a space between books. Miss Lathrop's red curls were especially animated today. The story was about a circus pony who'd gotten left behind by mistake when the circus moved on to the next town. He neighed and neighed but nobody paid him any attention, because the circus had been yesterday, and today everyone had things they had to do: go to work, go to school, mow the lawn, play with their toys. He trotted through the neighborhood, looking for his mother and the rest of the circus, sure there would be a clown behind the tree—! a trapeze artist resting on that bench—! the bearded lady waiting at the bus stop—!, and his hoofs made a ringing sound on the sidewalk, but nobody even looked up when he went past. After a while, he found himself in the countryside, where houses were fewer and farther between, and he realized he was tired and thirsty. He went up to a house and tapped his hoof on the welcome mat. A woman came to the door.

"What can I do for you?"

"I'm hot and thirsty and tired," he neighed, "and I miss my mother."

"Wait right here," she said, and he thought she was going to come back with his mother, but she only brought him a glass of water. "Here you go," she said.

He drank the water, which helped, but now he missed his mother more than ever.

Why not write a whole song, Larry thought. So what if he had never written a song before. He had never been a financial counselor before, either, but he knew you were supposed to pay off credit card debt, max your 401(k), buy low, sell high, and hang tight. As for what he knew about how to write a song: he knew what it was to be in love. What it was to be so in love that you were ready to place your life in someone else's hands.

Baby, baby, baby,
Don't say maybe.
Say yes! Oh, please!
I'm getting down on my knees
And I'm not getting up till you say,
"Okay."

He wanted to sing his song to Aileen right away, before he forgot the rhymes, so he reversed direction. What was work? He knew from personal experience that it was not the most important thing in life! Nobody ever fired a librarian! Besides, she would forgive him when she heard the song he had made up for her. She was too sweet not to forgive him. Behind him now was Picnic Point with its view of the state capitol, a dazzling tusk of a building, gleaming and white as if carved from ivory. Between the Point and the shore lay Lake Mendota, rippling water the brilliant toilet-bowl blue found in well-tended guest bathrooms.

There were always people on Picnic Point, but not often very many people. Couples, mostly, or a trio of friends, and people walking by themselves to escape the maddening crowd. The thick-boled trees were restful and their leaves dappled and dimmed the sunlight. As he walked back out of Picnic Point, he came face to face with the guy from the Job Fair.

"Were you following me?" Larry asked, stopping in front of him. They were about the same height.

"This is a public place. I have as much right as you to be here."

"Were you *following* me?"

"I was walking behind you. You can interpret that any way you like."

It was right about here that Larry understood he was talking with a meth head.

"Shit," Larry said. "If you don't stop following me I'll call a cop."

"I'm walking to the water's edge." At the water's edge, one could look to the right to see the west half of the university campus and the sailboats moored by the Student Union or turn slightly to the left to see the mental asylum. "Tell that to your cop."

Larry looked down and away and walked briskly back out of Picnic Point. Behind him the jerk yelled, "You got no *right* to go to a job fair, rich son'bitch like yourself!" He thought again about calling a cop, then figured he could play cat-and-mouse with a creep or sing his song to Aileen.

Aileen saw Larry out of the corner of her eye and then couldn't resist looking up at him. She flushed and bent her head back down over the book.

Larry thought she was beautiful, her curls dancing in front of her face, her elbows, scrubbed and vulnerable, showing below short sleeves, her feet in Dr. Scholl's sandals. She was surrounded by children.

Tavy pushed her face into the space she had been peering through. She was thinking how, if she had a pony, she would take good care of it and never, ever, forget and leave it behind when she went anywhere.

Tavy saw Larry Adcock come in and stand looking at Miss Lathrop. He was handsome, if old, but he stood there with his mouth hanging open, and she couldn't help thinking that if she had a spitball on hand, and if Miss Lathrop were not in the middle of a story, she'd like to try making a basket.

The man who came in behind him was weird-looking, his mouth closed so tight he almost didn't have lips. His eyes moved around so much it made her dizzy just to look at him. He was not someone she had ever seen before.

Then Tavy saw the gun and yelled.

Larry wheeled around. He saw the gun and dived in front of Aileen to protect her.

When he did that, Aileen saw the man behind him. She got up to put herself between the gunman and the children. If only she had studied karate instead of t'ai chi, but you could only do, in life, the best you could do with the tools you had, and what she had was t'ai chi, a gentle art of flexibility and alignment, at which she was none too good. She raised her right leg, and her sandaled foot caught Larry in the shoulder. He turned and grabbed at her waist as he came down, and the bullet directed at Larry hit her in the chest. She barely had time to see the blood blossoming on her blouse before she died.

In the brief instant during which Larry and Aileen faced each other, she managed to speak before she died. "Angel-kittens," she said.

Larry fell on top of her just as a bullet entered the back of his head. The last thing he heard was Aileen saying "angel-kittens." He knew she was referring to the children.

They lay there like lovers on stage at the end of a play by Shakespeare.

The children were wailing and screaming. Several of them were struck down, too, by the spray of shots that fanned the room, and two were killed instantly, a boy aged five and a boy aged four.

Gabe and Mike, Tavy learned later.

Tavy clapped her ears, because the gunshots were so loud that they made her head feel like someone was pounding on it with fists. The room smelled like something scorched on the stove, from all the gunsmoke, and she thought she might upchuck. But the gunman didn't see her behind the bookcase.

Someone came up behind the gunman and knocked the gun out of his hands and wrestled him down to the floor.

After that, there were ambulances and reporters and keening parents—an old story by now, and not one in which a pony ever finds his mother, a princess sleeps through the night, an elephant flies, or a train climbs over a hill. Tavy tucked a lock of her hair in her mouth and began sucking on it.

Tavy's mother tried to get her to talk. "Talking about it will make it easier," she said, holding her close, stroking the back of her head, coaxing her with Shel Silverstein and Dr. Seuss, pulling her onto her lap and rocking her even though they didn't have a rocking chair and once or twice the kitchen chair threatened to tip over backwards. But Tavy didn't want to talk—about what she had seen, or anything else. And how could she explain to her mother, whom she loved with all her being and would never actually want to trade for another, that she used to imagine Miss Lathrop taking over when her mother was dead, and that now she wondered if her thinking that had been why Miss Lathrop was killed? Miss Lathrop's being dead felt to her like a punishment for a sin she could never confess, because if she confessed it, her mother would be hurt. Her mother would think she had not been a good enough mother. For two months, Tavy refused to talk. It seemed the safest thing to do; she didn't want to say the wrong thing. She didn't talk about books at supper, and she didn't check out any new books from the library, although she did think about the lost pony sometimes at night before she went to sleep. "Don't be blue, sweetheart," her mother crooned, kissing her goodnight, but it was her mother who was blue, not her, except when she would think, *Poor little pony*. Lying in bed, she heard her parents whispering about her in the hallway. Her father told her mother that he was worried that she was "regressing." She figured out that he thought she was being babyish, which surprised her: couldn't he see how old she'd gotten inside?

Even wanting to let him know she was not "regressing" was not enough to get her to talk, but after a while she could see that her not talking was making her mother feel worse, not better, so finally she decided she'd better say something. She took her mother by the hand and led her to the big round dining table and asked her to sit down. She sat down herself. She had put on her brown-and-white seersucker jumper with acorn-shaped pockets for the occasion. She shoved her hands into the pockets and sighed heavily. She said, "I think Miss Lathrop was happy when Larry came in, because her face got almost as red as her hair, and she looked so pretty. I heard her say something before she died."

"What, honey?" The smile had gone out of her mother's voice.

"'Angel-kittens.' She said 'angel-kittens.' But she was reading a story about a pony, not about angel-kittens. I don't think there is a story with angel-kittens in it, do you? I've never read one, and I've read a lot of stories."

She had been trying to cheer her mother up, but now there were tears on her mother's face. She was sure her mother couldn't be crying about Larry and Miss Lathrop, because they were married and living happily ever after in heaven. It occurred to her that her mother might have read the circus pony story. Maybe she went to the library without Tavy and checked out the book Miss Lathrop was reading that day and, just like Tavy, it made her sad to remember how the pony had lain down in an open field at nightfall and gone to sleep without being tucked in. Being tucked in was one of the best things about being a kid, and if her *mom* could be in Miss Lathrop's story, she would tuck the pony in. "Mom, it's okay," she said, patting her mother comfortingly on the shoulder. "You have to remember it was just a story."

Shooting Star

When the baby was born, she would have fit in Roy's baseball mitt. He hadn't used that mitt since tenth grade; it needed oiling. It needed to be thrown away. In fact, he had thrown it away. But how could they throw their baby away? That was what the hospital said had to be done: their baby would die, and he and BB would have to bury or cremate their daughter, born at twenty-two weeks, ten point two ounces, bald but beautiful, with a delicate heartbreaking little cry that sounded like a kitten mewing. She was under a miniature plastic tent with a heat lamp to keep her warm.

When the baby died, BB felt she was being paid back for giving her first daughter away. It was God, perhaps, or more likely just the universe. Karma. BB did not believe she mattered enough in the great scheme for God to single her out and punish her, and yet she had committed a wrong and punishment was just. Apparently, the universe shifted its huge bulk now and again to get the kinks out. To compensate or rectify or equalize. It was obvious to her that their daughter's death had hit Roy like an Improvised Explosive Device. His eyes had been strafed and were bloodshot. He was holding his chest as if it had taken shrapnel. How could he not hate her? So she said, enunciating carefully, "If you're going to leave me because of this, do it now."

They had been prepared—the doctor had prepared them—but they were not prepared at all.

They had a private, silent funeral. No one was invited. No one spoke. A few days later BB answered the doorbell: the funeral home had messengered their daughter's ashes in a very small urn. They did invite their longtime friends Lola and Terry to the cemetery, where they interred the ashes, still in the small urn, in what looked like a cement safe in a wall of cement safes. Then they went to a bar for drinks. BB drank too much and threw up in the Ladies'. Roy tried hard to get drunk but stayed perplexingly sober. Lola and Terry bailed early, saying they had to get home to their kids.

In Mongolia, in Ulan Bator, a sky as blue as bluebirds flies over the Gobi Desert in the south and as far north as Siberia. The sky covers so much ground that one can become disoriented. The sun is omnipresent but cannot warm the ground except in July and August when the temperature rises to the low sixties.

Outside Ulan Bator, which has an air pollution problem, the air is clean and sweet and fresh, as gratifying to the palate as something to eat. The water is free of impurities.

BB and Roy's hotel was in the national park, some kilometers from the city. On the first day Roy met with his cinematographer, set designers, gofers, at the site he had selected. BB stayed in bed. It was almost noon when she got up.

She did her laps in the pool, toweled off, and dressed. Swimming had brought color into her face and made her eyes sparkle. She had that hair style where the roots are brown but her hair was blond.

Into the park, then, she went with picnic lunch packed by hotel staff. She marveled at the marmots—the staff had described them to her: furry little rodents resembling prairie dogs but not related to them. Russians had eaten marmots during famine and war. Now marmot was sometimes a specialty dish with spices and frou-frou.

She had never eaten squirrel and she wasn't going to eat marmot. They were adorable. They also carried bubonic plague, though she'd been assured that no one ever cooked a plague-ridden marmot.

She ate her sandwich while walking through the park. She popped the last bite into her mouth just as a man appeared beside her. "Hello," he said, though it sounded like *Herro*. "Such a beautiful park."

She swallowed as quickly as she could and said, "It is. It is a beautiful park."

"You are from America."

"How can you tell?"

"Your clothes."

"But I might have bought them in London. Or Paris or Rome." She was certain her clothes were international.

"No," he said. "American. Sporty."

She was wearing a lightweight aviator jacket, a tank, blue jeans, and Nikes.

"Do you fry a plane?" he asked, using his arms to steer an invisible wheel, which, of course, was not how to fly a plane.

She blushed. "No."

He was still walking beside her. His legs were long.

She felt duty-bound to break the silence, so she asked him if he was a Mongol, despite being sure he wasn't. She had already met several Mongols. He was taller, in a Western suit. And then there was the "r" for the "l."

"I was born in Japan," he said. "I travel for business. You, I think, are a tourist?"

"Some of the time." On days when she wasn't needed on set.

Other actresses studied drama in school. They learned Method or technique. They did summer theater or dinner theater. They memorized lines and knew how to cry on cue. They could discuss their "process." They built their characters. BB had no process, or rather, her process was to daydream. She would lie on her bed all morning, thinking about her character, imagining her character in different scenes—not just scenes that would be filmed but any scenes that occurred to her. She daydreamed her current character washing dishes, hiking mountains with her rifle slung over her shoulder, being made love to. She pictured her with a child, a husband, old and alone or dying young. She pictured her buying a quart of milk, teaching second graders, going to med school, gardening. She knew it would be a flower garden, not vegetables or herbs. She knew her character would achieve orgasm easily, that she would want to help sick people in a foreign land, that she poured milk on her cereal but never drank it from a glass. There was no system to any of this, nor was all of this information directly relevant, but it helped her to know her character and eventually the character was in her eyes, her face, her hands, her posture. She tried to feel what her character would feel, that's all. She had a mobile face, a passionate heart, an ear for speech rhythms.

"Have you attended the open-air market?"

"I just got here."

"I shall take you to the open-air market," he said.

Was he asking her on a date? She said, "I don't go on dates. I'm married." She had been with Roy since she was a teenager and had never felt marriage important. She did not know why she lied. Maybe she thought she needed hypothetical protection in case he was a maniacal serial killer.

"But you wear no ring."

She shrugged.

"I too am married," he said.

She glanced at his hand. "You wear no ring either."

"Men often do not wear a ring."

"So. It's the same with me."

"You are free tomorrow?"

"Yes."

"I shall get you at seven o'clock. We must go early. I wait for you in the lobby."

She nodded uncertainly. But it was only a trip to the open-air market.

Sometimes when BB was asleep in Roy's arms he turned so that she rolled into his armpit. Nor was it a smelly armpit—Roy kept himself clean and groomed himself with a certain amount of satisfaction—but with her nose pressed into it, she couldn't breathe. She would have to say, "I need air," and then he would turn to face the opposite direction, and she could turn on her own side, breathing freely. But then they might as well have been sleeping in separate beds, with separate dreams behind the closed curtains of their eyelids.

The next day Roy left at daybreak. BB had with her both her Stella McCartney handbag and a shopping bag made of twine and two sticks that she'd picked up in Poland.

He stood in the lobby—not pacing, as Roy would have, but standing without fidgeting, in the early light falling from the windows. The still light accentuated high, sharp cheekbones. He was slim. Lips full, fingers elegantly long. His skin a rosy yellow. When he turned toward her, she saw something in his eyes, but she couldn't decide what it was. Was it predatory? Was it delight? Was it a sense of superiority? And how could she see these disparate responses simultaneously in one man's glance?

She crossed the room, held out her hand to shake his.

"Good morning," he said. "My name is Takeo."

"I'm BB," she said.

He took her by the elbow and guided her to his car. A rented car, she thought.

"Now we are friends," he said, smiling. "Yes?"

The Terelj was a five-star hotel. She said to herself that a guest at a five-star hotel would not be a maniacal serial killer. She got into the car, fastening her seatbelt. "Yes." She smiled too.

The market was in the city, of which she now got a better look: wide streets, big buildings, Peace Avenue lined with beguiling boutiques. He found a parking place and they got out of the car, falling into step. *He is matching his step to mine*, she realized; *his would naturally be much longer*.

At the market—which, he told her, was also called the Farmers Market and the Black Market, and indeed there were, he said, black market dealings—there were currants, carrots, beets, and potatoes. Takeo explained that much food had to be imported because Mongolia's climate was so inhospitable to so many growing things.

But there was clothing, furniture, pottery. There were textiles and handmade jewelry. Beneath the ever-bright Mongolian sky, beneath the ever-present Mongolian sun, color flourished like flowers: red, green, blue, yellow, brown, orange. Color worn, color displayed, color carried in the shopping bags of men and women. Perhaps not outside the city, where the brown earth was pointillistic with white sheep, where the monotone steppes extended to the edge of the world, but BB believed she had never seen so much color in her life as here, now, in Ulan Bator. Was it cheerful? Charming? This manifestation of local color? Or not so local—Takeo explained that many goods, as well as foods, were imported from China. She felt as if she were at the center of a monstrous paisley panoply, except that it was always impossible to find a center in paisley. She felt overwhelmed. It was similar to the feeling she had when they first arrived: as if there were nothing on either side to stop her from toppling over. But here there was all this *stuff* on either side—why did she feel just the opposite? It must be the sky again. She stopped in her tracks and stood looking down.

"Are you okay?" he asked. He touched her lightly on the shoulder.

She kept her eyes down, as if she were a nun practicing custody of the eyes. She had once played a nun. "I need a glass of water or something."

He led her to a yurt tucked into a side street.

"Everything smells like lamb," she said.

"Almost everything in this country is mutton. You'd like shashlik. It is rather like shishkabob."

"Just water, please."

The owner brought water.

"People speak English here? Not just in the hotel?"

"Many do. The Soviet Union—kaput." She found it interesting to hear a Japanese use German to speak to an American in Mongolia. "Now they learn English."

She searched his face, although she could not have said for what. "My husband and I are here to make a movie. A film."

"Ahso," he said. "This explains your beauty."

She ignored his compliment. "This country is a moonscape," she said.

"Maybe a Mars-scape," he said, his eyes focused on her and smiling.

"Does Mars have mountains?"

He pantomimed his lack of knowledge. "Your film, what is it about?"

"Warring tribes. Modern warring tribes. I play a doctor who is held hostage by bandits. I kill one of my kidnappers, seize his Kalashnikov, and escape."

"Velly exciting," he said.

"Not so much," she said. "But I like being on location. Seeing different parts of the world."

"Those who travel are often looking for themselves."

She wouldn't have him lecturing her. "I travel for work. Like you."

"Of course," he said, knowing that he'd been reprimanded. "You are private."

Leaving the yurt, he took her hand. In a light, loose way, but why was she compliant, she asked herself. Because, she answered herself, he was treating her as if she were a real person. She was used to thinking of herself as an image made of light cast on a screen. In other words, as next to nothing.

Not to Roy, of course. He did not think she was a mere image.

And yet, wasn't an image exactly what he needed her for?

Not that she objected. She wasn't a firebrand. She was pliable. And she liked being pliable.

The sun was overhead. Takeo said, "Let us go to lunch. You must be hungry, as am I."

"I should get back to the hotel," she said.

"Is your husband waiting for you?"

She shook her head.

"Then let us eat in the hotel. It has several restaurants."

They had drinks, and more drinks. BB inspected him across the table. His face was handsomely ascetic. Rarely was she in the presence of a man without Roy. Not that he would mind, but she was used to spending her time with him or alone. She had girlfriends, but they were married. *And had children.*

Takeo's fingers were long and she imagined them touching her. Her arm, the back of her neck, her hair. And then her face, and then her breasts, and then—

She didn't know why she was flirting with this idea. But sex was less frequent now, as she and Roy were afraid of another pregnancy and just as afraid of not succeeding at another pregnancy. The two possibilities canceled each other, just like nuclear war. It seemed to her that these days they handled each other with kid gloves. Less frequent? How about nonexistent? When the waiter cleared their dishes from the table, Takeo ordered cognac for both of them. He was trying to get her drunk, she thought: well, then, she'd get drunk. He would escort her to his room and when they unlocked the door he would invite her in. That's what this was leading to. She heard her body saying *yes*. Probably he could hear it too. She imagined his hands between her legs. She felt her body heating up—"hotting" up, teenagers said these days. She reached across the table to touch his left cheekbone, the cliff-edge of it, the Verrazano Bridge of it. She could imagine herself, a miniature version of herself, balancing on the edge of his cheekbone and throwing herself off, off, off into the hurtling dark water below. Or like Sigourney Weaver into the fire in *Alien: Resurrection*. Which had not been very good except for that scene, but that scene was amazing. She felt reckless, mesmerized, and ready. He caught her reaching arm and gently set it down on the table but said nothing about it.

He walked her to *her* room. He stood at the door while she unlocked it. He said *Sayonara* and walked away.

She missed him. Already she missed him and he'd been gone only a minute.

Two minutes.

Three.

He stayed gone. She decided she had misinterpreted everything. And why was she disappointed? Did she really want to risk what she and Roy had had for so long?

Roy was in the room. He stripped off his shirt, then his pants, which he left on the floor. He turned on the shower. He was whistling "We're Off to See the Wizard, the Wonderful Wizard of Oz." She heard the water turn off. Roy returned from the shower with wet hair, a towel coiled around it like a Sikh turban, another towel around his waist. At that point he said Hi. From the doorway of the bathroom hot, humid air poured into the bedroom.

BB brought him a clean shirt, clean underwear, clean pants, clean socks, and a belt from the dresser drawer. She watched him putting them on. "Thanks, honey," he said.

"I met a man," she announced. "Japanese."

He raised his eyebrows.

"We went to the open-air market."

"Good for you! I'm glad you're seeing some of the city."

"He said we should try shashlik. It's a Russian dish."

"Fine, let's try it. I'm afraid I've been sticking to cheeseburgers." He thought. "And they're sticking to me," he said, slapping his abdomen, which was really quite trim for a man his age. He was well into his forties. "Where do you want to eat?"

"I have to admit," she said, "I'm not really hungry."

"Honey, we're in Ulan Bator. Short of a sequel, it's probably the only time we'll ever be here. Let's go dancing." He got up and did a quick . . . a quick *something*. The Chicken or the Wave or the Macarena. It was hard to tell, with him.

She relented. "Okay, we'll go dancing." She wondered how Mongols danced.

The shashlik was excellent. But the hotel clientele was international and at least at this time of night, at least this night, they restricted themselves to slow dancing. She leaned her head on Roy's shoulder; he had his hand on her back. They swayed together, mostly in the same spot. *The story of my life*, she thought, but without resentment, because it had been a good life so far. It wasn't just that Roy protected her, took care of her, looked out for her. He was courtly. He still held doors open for her, still made a production of her birthdays. But it wasn't just that, either. It was that he made no attempt to direct her life. It was that he listened to her. In fact, he was perfect, except—

Except all sex had ceased.

She wondered if Roy felt the least inclination toward sex. And would he ever again? There was no longer any sexual tension with him. With her head on her husband's shoulder, she wondered what it would be like to be dancing with Takeo.

That night she fell asleep on her side of the outrageously wide bed. Roy was so far away he seemed unreachable.

She woke up at 1:45 in the morning. The room was dark, Roy for once not snoring. She rose and went to the window, hiding behind the curtain as she looked out. She had never cheated on Roy. She had never wanted to. Now she wanted to.

For that matter, she wanted to scream, to hurl things, smash things, reach inside herself and yank out her heart and throw that away with the rest of her stupid life.

He stirred when she climbed back into bed. He rolled toward her and they slept front to back, two spoons in the bowl of the bed.

For several days, not being needed for filming, BB joined Takeo to see the sights of Mongolia. In the mornings, after Roy left, she dressed and went to the lobby. Staff brought her a cup of coffee. By the time she finished it, Takeo was there.

"Where today?" he asked at the end of the week.

"Orkhon Khurkhree, please." It was on the hotel's list of things to see.

"Good," he said. "We shall go. Bring bathing suit."

"Why?"

"You'll see."

It would be a long trip. He held the passenger door of his rental car open and she slid in.

They drove in silence at first, passing Soviet-era apartment buildings that were returning to rubble and Mongolian *ger* compounds, the tent communities that suited life in the desert so much better than permanent buildings. After a while she said, "Tell me about yourself."

"There is nothing to tell."

"Where in Japan were you born? Are your parents living? Do you have brothers and sisters? Where did you go to school? Did you go to college? What is your business? What is your favorite color? Do you like ice cream? Do you have a pet? Children?"

"You require many answers," he said, plainly amused.

"I do," she said. "Begin."

He told her that he was born in Kyoto, the "most beautiful, historical, and cultural city" in his country; that his mother was elderly but alive; that he had a brother who was an engineer in Michigan; that he had done his baccalaureate at the Sorbonne; that he worked for the World Health Organization; that his favorite color was red; his favorite ice cream was pistachio; he had no pet and no children.

They drove around a small group of tourists riding camels, and soon they were well into the countryside—mountains pasted against the gigantic sky like postage stamps, ox carts and sheep herders occasionally on the road but thinning out, the road occasionally difficult to distinguish from dry earth. Occasionally also, they passed a goat picking through garbage. They stopped to let a flock of sheep cross the road. They kept the windows up, because if they opened them, they were besieged by flies. They spotted another goat and then another.

Shouldn't the broad expanse of blue be exhilarating? Yesterday, BB had been exhilarated by the thin air. Today she was overcome by a sense of her insignificance. Surely the inhabitants of this land were overmatched by the landscape, swallowed up by it. It made everything small by comparison. She thought Mongols must be in a continuous state of defeat, despite their history of Chinggis Khaan (she liked this authentic form of the name) and the Mongol Empire. She wondered how anyone in Mongolia could exert sufficient strength to do anything, because, next to this landscape, it would be ineffectual and therefore pointless.

"In Mongolia," Takeo said, as if reading her mind, "one should not say anything negative. The people are superstitious and think that to say something negative is to guarantee bad fortune."

Takeo turned on the radio. Mongolian pop music blared. He hit the side of his thumb against the steering wheel in time with the music. She settled down and stared out the window. Some water would be good, she thought, and as soon as she thought it, Takeo handed her a bottle of spring water. So she stared out the window while gulping water. It was not cold but it quenched her thirst.

Takeo turned the radio down and said, "Also you must not whistle indoors. Another superstition." He turned the radio back up.

Poor Roy, she thought. Had he already brought bad fortune on himself? She hoped not.

They came to Orkhon Khurkhree. She followed Takeo to the edge of the cliffs. "Most pretty," he said.

"Beautiful," she agreed. A natural wonder, she thought. An accidental miracle. She felt spray on her face—or was she imagining it? She smelled the waterfall as if it were an unimaginably large flower or as if the falling water were actually vines of wisteria, blue and sweet and enchanting and soothing. She wished she could get in a tub full of this water.

"Water so chirry," Takeo said, pulling up his jacket collar and shivering to emphasize his point. "But tourists swim anyway. Mongols do not like to swim."

It was hard to hear him over the crashing noise of the falls. She turned her hearing aid up. He was saying that the two of them would swim later.

Watching the water fall over the cliff and crash and churn in the pool below, BB thought how peculiar the world was. It wasn't just Mongolia. Everywhere, fire and water brought good and evil, while earth and air persuaded us to cling to our planet. Yet that might change. Someday, humans might find themselves waking up in another world. Someday, humans might slide down (would there be a "down"? an "up"?) a worm hole to emerge in another galaxy, and the other galaxy would be just as peculiar as this one.

A galaxy or a *ger*. Takeo took her to a white-felt-tented store in which there was a small restaurant. He ordered a cheese drink for her and salty tea for himself, but she couldn't get the cheese drink down. She knew good Mongolian manners meant she had to taste it at least, but she set it aside after a sip. The worker who had brought it to her seemed happy with that. He went away and came back with a can of Coke.

Takeo took her to a second *ger*. "After we swim," he said, "we can stay here."

Did he mean overnight?

"I have to be back at the hotel by seven," she said.

"It is fine. No problem."

There was a small stove in the *ger*. "For the nights," he said.

She started to say again that she had to be back at seven, but he smiled and said, "Yes, I know, seven." Then he left the *ger*, indicating that she should change into her bathing suit.

The water at the base of the fall shocked her with its coldness but soon she was acclimated and they played with a large plastic ball he had brought. Square shoulders, six-pack-abs, those long legs—and did he carry a large plastic ball wherever he went? Was he prepared at all times to go swimming? He'd purchased it at the open-air market, he said when they climbed ashore. Her hair was plastered to her face, her face rosy with exercise and high spirits and his gaze. All at once she felt self-conscious and tried to hide. But it is difficult to hide in a bathing suit. He pulled her arms away from her chest. "Most pretty," he said again, kissing her on the tops of her breasts, kissing her mouth as if he had every right to do that. And hadn't she given him that idea, she thought? If she stopped him, he would be furious. Did she want him to stop? No. She didn't think so. She wasn't sure. He carried their few things to the car, and she followed, knowing that she was in too deep to get out.

In their *ger* again, he said, "Sit, please," motioning toward the bed/couch.

"Oh—" she started, but he put his hand over her mouth.

"Shhh," he said. "Nothing negative."

Someone called his name from outside. "He is asking me to tether the dog," Takeo explained. BB looked wildly around the *ger*. There was no dog.

"It means he is here."

"Who?" She was still looking for a dog.

"He who is bringing to us our vodka." Takeo stepped out outside and returned with vodka and glasses.

He poured a shot for each of them.

"*Kampai!*" he said, draining his glass in one go. She followed suit.

The man who brought vodka had also brought cold salami and green onions.

Takeo was lying on the bed—or couch—and she sat cross-legged facing him, the food between. He stripped a green onion and teased her lips with it until she opened her mouth and took it between her teeth. "You rike," he said, and laughed. Up close, his high cheekbones seemed to her to have been sculpted from marble, his forehead high and smooth. They did two more shots apiece and then he pulled her down on top of him. When she kissed him he tasted of salami and onion. Animal smells, earthy flavors, and now she wanted more and more from his mouth. He stopped for a moment to move the food and drink off the bed, or was it a couch? When he turned back to her, he pulled off her cargo pants, her sweater, everything. She felt her skin was on fire. She had never been so hot. Or had she just forgotten?

He was putting on a condom.

She moved his hand away. "No condom," she said.

He stopped. "I must."

"You must? Don't be silly. I don't have HIV, for heaven's sake. Or anything else. You know you'll like it better without."

"Not I," he said. He had moved off her and pulled a blanket over them.

She sat up. "Why not?"

"You are married. Suppose you get pregnant."

"It wouldn't be your responsibility."

"I cannot to fuck without rubber."

She grabbed her clothes. He caught her by the arm. "You wish to become pregnant."

She shook him off and put on her clothes.

"It is your husband's responsibility," he said.

On the ride back, they had nothing to say to each other. BB kept her face to the window. Wildflowers were so plentiful one might wrongly assume they had been planted. Their colors caught the eye.

I'd rather not go out this evening," she said.

"We have to eat."

"We can order room service."

"Is something the matter?"

"No."

"Did you see your friend today?"

"We went to see the most amazing waterfall."

Roy said nothing for a moment. Then: "He seems to have a lot of free time."

"He's taking meetings. That leaves him a lot of free time."

"I have the impression that you've been spending a lot of *your* time with him."

"I have. He's a good guide."

"Well," Roy said. "Was the waterfall really amazing?"

"Yes."

"Maybe I should go see it."

"Do," she said. "It really is amazing."

Roy put a finger under her chin and raised her head until her eyes met his. "You're tired?"

"I am," she said.

He kept looking at her. She met his gaze evenly.

"Then you won't mind if I go out?"

"No," she said, but as soon as the door closed behind him, tears brimmed her eyes.

In the morning she had to be on the set with Roy. He went through the scene with her. She had to run toward the camera while the camera rolled backward ahead of her. The whole time they were shooting BB thought about Takeo's insistence on the condom and her reluctance. She thought about his vertigo-inducing cheekbones, his accomplished hands, about the way he'd knocked back the vodka, his black hair flung back, his prominent Adam's-apple. Men's Adam's-apples were sexy; they differentiated the sexes as much as anything else.

Roy called a halt to the action. He came up to her. "You're not thinking about why you're running," he pointed out. "You're frightened but determined. And not just for your own sake. People are depending on you."

An assistant spritzed her face. Another assistant moussed her hair.

Roy touched his fingers to her lips. "You can do this, sweetie," he said. "Just put your mind to it."

She remembered having imagined her character as a woman whose child was drowning, the look on the imagined woman's face as she ran to the edge of the beach. The next take went smoothly. When it was over, she retired to the trailer she shared with Roy. He was still shooting. She didn't want to talk with anyone. She wanted to think about how quickly being in the *ger* with Takeo had changed from romantic to sexual to angry. The three stages of something, though she didn't know what. Divorce?

It was foolish to have a trailer here, she thought. Instead of a trailer, they should have had a *ger*. When in Mongolia, one should do as Mongols do. She wanted to ride one of the small, sturdy, famed Mongolian horses before she left. She wanted to see the Gobi Desert. Would there be time? Time was in Roy's hands; he knew their schedule, the costs, their obligations to their backers, cast, and crew.

She went out with Roy that night to a place where Mongolian art was displayed and throat-singers sang. A Mongol poet recited a poem in Mongolian and then in English translation. Or maybe the poem was by someone else and he was simply performing it. She wasn't sure. The restaurant was crowded and rife with chatter and even with her hearing aid on she couldn't always hear everything.

Roy talked about his film, how he wanted it to have the mountainous terrain, the horizon, of Mongolia and the dangerous intricacy of Afghanistan, how he wanted it to move people and make them think. BB had heard this before but she was content to let him run on while she thought her own thoughts. He was talking about the day's rushes when she found herself interrupting. "Let's get married," she said.

"Why?" he asked. They had been together a quarter of a century.

"Because I want to. Because I need to. Do you have an objection?"

"No," he said, "but why now?"

"I want a ring on my finger."

He leaned back in his chair. "This has something to do with your Japanese friend, doesn't it."

"Yes," she admitted.

"You've seen a lot of him."

"Yes."

"Did you sleep with him?"

"No."

"Are you telling the truth?"

"Yes," she said.

"Do you want to tell me more about what's going on in your head?"

"No."

He finished his decaf, black, and signaled for the waiter, placing his credit card on the table.

"When and where?" he asked.

"Here and now."

"What's the hurry?"

"I can't live without you. You must know that."

"That's not true. I'm more tied to you than you are to me."

She shrugged. "The difference is miniscule."

"Are you sure you want to do this?"

"Yes."

The waiter came back with the credit card and the receipt, which Roy signed.

"You really want to get married here?"

"Why not? It will surprise the hell out of Lola and Terry." She tried to sound cheerful but her voice broke and she said, "And maybe, on our wedding night, we can have sex. What do you think?"

"I've wanted not to hurt you," he said. "I didn't want to make you have sex if you didn't want it. You've been so sad."

"I want it. Besides, we love each other. How can getting married hurt anything?"

The Wedding Palace on Marx Street was not far off the main square, Sukhbaatar Square, from which one could see the four sacred mountain peaks. During the Soviet era the Wedding Palace had been strictly secular but now religious marriages were permitted. Roy and BB, however, felt no compulsion for a religious ceremony. Their faith was in their affection for each other. Roy wore jeans and a silk shirt; BB wore a curve-fitting, below-the-knee dress by St. John. Witnesses were the cameraman and the Justice's secretary, a Mongol woman who knew some English. When the ceremony was over, the cameraman bought them a drink at a bar.

When they came out of the bar, someone on the square was singing a "long song," in which each word is held so long that a complete song might be only a handful—a small spoonful—a pinch—of words. The cameraman took off, and BB and Roy listened to the singing for a while. "If you could write a song with ten words, what would they be?" Roy asked her.

"Blue pears, God's heart, words like wild ponies, man, woman."

"Why did we wait so long to do this?"

"We didn't want things to change. They changed anyway."

He put a silk-sleeved arm around his wife. "Promise you won't meet any more Japanese men."

She slipped out from under his arm, hopped off the bench, and knelt before him. "Honey," he said, "what are you doing? Get back up here."

"I have to be on my knees to say this, Roy."

He glanced around to see if anyone were watching.

"Nobody here knows who we are," she said. "It doesn't matter what they think." On her knees, she said, "I want you to know that I have loved you since forever and always will and I will always be faithful to you."

"Do you think I don't already know that?" he asked. "Get up now, please."

"One more thing." She had her hearing aid on and could hear the traffic on Peace Avenue and a jet overhead. She took her eyes away from Roy's for a moment to see the contrail, white in all that overwhelming blue. Not for the first time she thought how amazing it was that people everywhere live their local lives amid such immensities of time and space. She and Roy were leaving in the morning. She turned her glance back to him, locking her eyes with his. "What about children?"

"Children," he said meditatively, and it seemed to her that the end of the whole of history might arrive before he continued. Then he smiled. "Someone has to have them," he said. He spread his arms wide as if to embrace millions.

The Autobiography of My Mother(s)

I'm no writer, so I'll just stick to the facts.

My mother is a writer, and she's always twisting the facts, or blurring them, or screwing with them. I guess that's Fact #1.

Fact #2: She's a great mom and I love her.

Fact #3: My mom is also my great-aunt.

I call her Nina now that I'm a grown up and have a daughter of my own. Nina is sixty-eight. She adopted me when I was a brand-new baby, and a consequence of that adoption is what I want to set down here: *factually*.

When I asked Nina who my birth mother was, she answered, "A very pretty young woman."

I was fourteen before Nina mentioned that my birth mother was her niece. Her brother's daughter.

"What was he like?" I asked then. "Your brother?"

"Complicated," she said. I don't know anybody who isn't complicated, so that didn't tell me much.

"Did you know my father?"

"He stayed here briefly. There's nothing much I can tell you about him. His name was Roy."

I pictured him on horseback.

"Roy Dante."

I pictured him riding a horse into an inferno.

Not a lot of help, right?

Writing about Nina, I'll try to be more helpful. Because there are things people should know about her. Things a critic or biographer ought to know.

When she was little, she was shy. She once ate dinner under the table because she was too shy to let herself be seen. Her parents had guests over. She got under the table, reached out a hand, and her mother served her a plate. Hushpuppies, grits, squash, and ham, but I think she just made that part up in her writerly, fact-changing way, because who would remember a menu from when they were four?

Nina learned to give readings—in her late thirties—and mix with people, but her natural inclination was to shut herself up in a room to read or write. I guess that's true of most writers. Me, I like blasting the walls with music or hanging with friends while I paint. You'd think writers would be the verbal ones and painters would never open their mouths, but no. Maybe writers absorb so many words from reading that they have to go off by themselves to figure out which words they've got are actually theirs and not somebody else's. I mean, I've always read a lot too, but I also have other things to do.

So, anyway: shy, but kind of brave, too, because she fought a war with her shyness and came out the winner. What else? Ambitious. She didn't let on about that—at least not the full extent of it, not to most people—but I remember things she used to tell me. How she wanted to be—would be—a *great* writer. And how this was not, exactly, ambition, because it was just the truth, and that she didn't care about acclaim because being great was not about having people admire you and sing your praises, it was about making something that would bring aesthetic happiness into the world. I asked her what she meant by "aesthetic happiness." "It's what happens when you feel so fully and deeply that if you don't share it you'll burst. It's what makes a person an artist." I knew exactly what she meant.

Aesthetic happiness. Not happy-happiness. Something fuller and deeper. Something that spills over.

She no longer talks about being a great writer. Instead she likes to say she'll be a footnote to a footnote to a forgotten writer. Yet I have no doubt that she still nurtures her ambition. She figures that at her age people will think it's inappropriate, so she's learned to hide it. But she still believes she'll do it. Be a great writer.

Of course we sometimes fought, especially when I was a teenager. My mother was naturally girly. She was all about clothes and cosmetics and so forth. My mother is two generations away from me, odd as that sounds, and maybe she isn't as liberated as I am. Who gives a shiitake about clothes? Why would any woman make her face a lie? She would get after me about combing my hair or try to coax me into trying a little eye shadow or she'd criticize my wardrobe. "You can't just have jeans in your closet," she said to me, once. "What is wrong with you?" That hurt. Jeans are convenient and comfortable, and hardly anybody wears anything else. There was nothing wrong with me. The only parties I wanted to go to were parties where people wore jeans. Plus, I have cargo pants in my closet, too.

Another time, my mother bought a "styling wand" and told me to use it on my hair. "Why?" I asked. "So it will look intentional!" she said.

"Intentional hair? That's what you want me to have?"

"Intended hair," she said. "*A*-ttended hair."

I shoved the styling wand to the back of my closet and she never asked me about it again. Nina had her worries about me but she didn't really try to change me and she always had my back. If anybody said something unkind to me, she was on it like Jack Bauer in *24*. When some boys stole what my mother called my safety dollar from me, she made sure they returned it with a nickel interest. And when I acted up, she'd scold me but at the same time tell me how much I mattered to her and that she wanted me to be happy. When I was a child, she took me to the library every week to check out books, and when I was older, she drove me to art lessons.

She married Palmer when I was five. He was *Dad* to me. Palmer would take me to the university with him every year on Bring a Child to Work Day. He had a posh office overlooking Lake Mendota. That time of year the chances are it's still cold in Madison. The lake would have unfrozen, but leaves on trees were tentative. From his office I could see Picnic Point, where we sometimes went for walks on weekends. The lake was blue and choppy, not many boats on it yet, the insane asylum on the other side. I thought it was funny that the insane asylum and the English Department faced each other, but when I told Palmer that, all he said was "Ah." I would look through his books with prints of medieval paintings but in the beginning I just played with his stapler or curled under his desk to play peek-a-boo. I still remember the smell of his shoes from those afternoons—leather and polish. One of those days I tied his shoelaces together while he was reading and he tripped when he tried to stand up. I cried, because I hadn't meant to hurt him. He made me sit on the couch. He had a small blue couch in the office. I sat as still as I could for what seemed like hours, but he said it was ten minutes. That couldn't have been true, though, because I had taken the opportunity to count to infinity. I counted for a long, long time, until I could see that there would always be one more number, and after that I would count "one, two, three, four, five, six, seven, eight, nine, ten and so on to infinity."

When I got knocked up I told Nina I didn't want to have an abortion or put the baby up for adoption. I knew how long she waited to be a mom, and I wanted to take the opportunity while I had it. I told her I wouldn't marry Zayed even if he asked me. She wanted me to tell her about him, so I did. "He's from Nigeria and he wears do-rags and an earring in both ears and he's so hot that just looking at him made me feel—" I realized I didn't want to say *sexual*. I said *tropical*. She nodded, as if she understood, but I don't think she really did: the feeling of wanting to crawl on top of him, lick his face, pull his pants down. Like he's lean and hard-bodied, and you could play washboard blues on his pecs and abs. Oh, I was crazy with lust, I wanted to eat him with a spoon. Until he brought Jewel to one of the parties. I said, "Why are you with her?" He kissed me on the cheek and laughed. "Baby, it's not like we're married," he said. "We're just having a good time." So I told him I was pregnant. "That's impossible," he said. "You're on the Pill, aren't you?"

I should have been. Of course I should have been. Nina had made sure that I had a prescription while I was still in high school. Who knows, maybe I subconsciously wanted to get pregnant so I wouldn't end up having to adopt my niece's baby when I was forty. I was ashamed to confess to Zayed that I wasn't on the Pill. I just gave him a mean look and walked away from the party.

I saw him around here and there, and a couple of times he tried to phone me but I wouldn't take his calls and he stopped. Hadn't we loved the same things: visual art, music, literature? I was working on my M.F.A. in painting. We were in the same French class and practiced speaking it with each other. *Je t'aime.* Who pulls your head close to his chest and whispers that in your ear just to try it out? In the hallways I held my head high, you can be sure of that.

Sometimes I want to be with someone who is neither a parent nor a child. Is that a terrible thing to admit? I want to go to a bar and drink and talk painting half the night and go home with a man. Or come back here and paint until the sun comes up. Sometimes I *do* go to a bar and drink and go to a man's apartment but not very often and I always come home to this basement. I want to be here for my daughter.

I want to take a trip out of my life—a week, a weekend, someplace where no one has a cold or a fever or homework, where no one is practicing or painting or writing or reading medieval history. Rome or Paris or New York. Maybe I would go to Nigeria—Zayed wouldn't be there; he's in Denver with his MBA and his wife, I hear—but I would absorb all the bright, fierce colors of woven fabrics and learn about Callie's ethnic ancestry.

California? California seems like a place for phonies—people pretending they are other people.

Nina and Palmer said the baby and I could live with them until I earned enough money to move out. My parents fixed up the basement for us. I went to my classes right up to when the baby was due and returned to them right after.

Okay, so here we are, Callie and I, in the basement. They've never told us to get out though once Nina and Palmer and I thought it would be a temporary situation. Lucky for me, my parents don't see an artist as an irresponsible non-maturing adult mooching off of them. They understand that I work hard at being an artist. I still wear jeans all the time though Callie has some very cool little dresses, the kind that should be called frocks. She loves her frocks. And any little piece of jewelry or a barrette. But I digress. So we live in the basement here, and about a year ago the phone rings, the landline upstairs. By the time I get to it Nina's come down from the second floor and she's already got it, the receiver pressed to her left ear and she's got her right hand over her mouth as if she's preventing herself from speaking and she's looking at the living room but there are tears in her eyes. She blinks and two tears fall simultaneously, one down each side of her face, and catch at the corners of her mouth. I wait until she hangs up with a faint "goodbye" and then I sink down next to her on the sofa. "That was your birth mother," she says, whereupon my throat turns to broken glass and I know that anything I say is going to hurt me.

"She's in California."

I wait.

"She's an actress. She lives with your father."

They're together? And they still didn't want me? I had assumed that they broke up, went separate ways, she regretting the loss of her child, he callously indifferent to what he'd done. I'd spent a lot of time during high school imagining where my mother was and what she might be doing. Probably back home with her mother to finish school. Working at Wal-Mart or Dairy Queen. Maybe she took a business course. I never dreamed she'd be an actress.

And knowing she was still with my father, and making a good living, I wondered why they hadn't cared enough to come back for me, or at least ask Nina about me. I wasn't a toy. I wasn't a Pixar character. I was *real.*

"He's a film director."

Nina's vocabulary grows stranger and stranger. "They were recently on location," she says.

"Location?" A word has taken the daredevil move of leaving my mouth.

"In Mongolia."

She's not making any sense. I say, "No," and go back downstairs. My daughter is at her violin lesson. Soon I need to start cooking dinner for her.

Nina comes to the head of the stairs. "I think she wants to make it up with you," she says.

"Too late!" I call up. "I'm twenty-six!" Remember, this was a year ago. "I have a daughter of my own!"

"You can explain that to her when she gets here tomorrow."

I lie down on my single bed and try to take it all in. It's too soon, I think. Twenty-six years is much too soon.

I was curious, of course. Not to say this wasn't a shock, but if it hadn't happened it might not have been long before I went looking for *her*, simply because another twenty-six years would be a really long time.

Callie was at school when Nina got back from picking up my other mother at the airport. I didn't go because the Madison airport is small enough that when you're in it, you can see everyone who's there. I didn't want anyone to see *me*.

So they arrive home and Nina hollers to me to come up. I do, and looking at my birth mother is like looking in a mirror except she's kempt, and I am now and forever unkempt. Also, she's blonde; I'm not. Also, she's a knock-out; I'm not. But otherwise, we could be twins. If I, like her, had a hairdresser, a makeup artist, and a trainer.

"Tavy," says my almost-mirror-image. "I'm BB."

"As in French?" I ask.

She seems surprised by my question and when she answers, she stumbles over her words. "My initials. I was born Babette Bryant but now I'm BB."

"Why?" I ask, although this whole conversation seems tangential.

She thinks so too and says, "I'm so happy to meet you," her face beatific in a way mine would never be.

I know I'm supposed to say "I'm happy to meet you" back but I don't. I don't feel happy, just confused. She drops her eyes for a moment. Light cups around her head like a hand that wants to protect her. I say the words. "I'm happy to meet you too."

She smiles. I mean, she's *radiant*.

"Why didn't my father come with you?" I can contemplate her compelling beauty or I can get down to brass tacks. I choose the brass tacks.

"He's editing a film, plus we thought you might feel smothered if we both came."

"Or he wants you to give him a report before he gets mixed up in this."

"Tavy," Nina says, signaling I should mind my manners. But *why* should I mind my manners? I don't owe this strange woman a thing. Oh, right. The strange woman gave birth to me.

"Okay," says BB, "I lied. He's not here because he doesn't know I'm here."

"Why the secrecy?"

"I didn't know how you'd feel about seeing me. I don't even know how he'll feel about my having seen you."

"You don't know much."

"Tavy." From Nina again, this time with more threat behind it.

"I know," BB says. "I know I don't know much. But you're my daughter and I wanted to see you. That's all I know."

"Nina's my real mother," I say, at the same time remembering my amazement meeting Callie when she came out of my body. You're my *daughter*, I thought, holding her; you're *my* daughter. I can see that BB must have felt something like that, but for Callie and me that had only been the beginning of our mother- and daughter-hood.

BB smiled even more brightly. Her teeth looked as if they'd been manicured. "I would just like us to be friends."

"Friends," I repeated, but as a query, not a statement.

Nina had opened a bottle of Chardonnay and was pouring it into the special wine glasses she'd found in a used-thingamajig shop on the Upper East Side in New York. In their shallow bowls, the wine drew light to it, as if each glass were a miniature pond.

BB moved back into the couch, retreating. I had the familiar feeling of having won, followed by the familiar feeling of "Won what?"

"Let me tell her," Nina said to BB. She took a seat on the ancient Green Bay Packers chair.

"Tell me what?" I asked.

I could tell something was coming. My voice climbed a little higher. My instinct was to hold my body in place, to stay close to it, as if it were about to be taken from me.

"Babette—BB—had a baby who died."

Shock on shock, that's for sure.

Of course I feel a rush of pity. I try to imagine what it would be like if Callie died, but it's impossible, because without her I would no longer be me and the world would be irrelevant, or rather, black and beyond painting. Then, not knowing I'm going to say it, I say, "I am not going to be a substitute for anybody's baby." This astounds me because I don't know where it comes from.

"That's not what—" BB began, but she broke off and instead turned to Nina.

"I shouldn't have come, Nina. I'm sorry."

And I'm sorry too, and even cringe a bit, ashamed. But somebody should understand: I felt blindsided. I didn't mean to drive her away; I just wanted her to understand that I have my own life and it's one in which I'm not her child. And though she doesn't have me, she does have a grandchild. That's pretty big.

"I'm sorry for Tavy's lack of manners," Nina said.

"Shouldn't you be defending me?" I said to Nina.

"You're so good at defending yourself," she said. "Sweetie, it hasn't been long since the baby—" She stopped, then said, "Died."

"It's horrible that the baby died. But— You didn't tell her about Callie, did you," I said, turning from Nina to BB.

"Tell me what?" BB asked.

"That you're a grandmother."

"Me? I'm a grandmother?" BB halfway jumps up from the couch, then drops into it again, her eyes wide and her face blank, as if she doesn't want to accept what I said until she's sure of it.

I nod, though I'll grant she didn't look like anybody's grandmother.

"I have a six-year-old daughter. I got pregnant at twenty and decided to keep the baby. *Keep* the baby."

"You were old enough," she said. "I was fourteen. There's an immeasurable difference between fourteen and what did you say? Nineteen? Twenty? You were an adult."

I wouldn't have said I was an adult, but I see BB's point.

Just then Callie turned up in the room. Sometimes she'll just soundlessly slip into a room. She's not sneaky, just by nature elegant and composed. Which is not to say she's not a kid. And her curly hair does make her noticeable. She looks like an African American—and much prettier—Little Orphan Annie.

Callie, quiet and inward, stopped short in front of BB. She stared at BB. "You must be Tavy's daughter," BB said. It did not take a genius to figure that out.

"Come here, honey," I told her. She had her first-grade reader in hand and she held it out sideways to me, still staring at BB.

"Callie, say hello to BB," Nina said. "She's—your other grandmother."

My child was wearing a seersucker sun dress with green and white checks and white sandals. Seersucker had just been revived and Callie spotted the dress in a store and begged for it.

"Hi," Callie whispered to BB, being more polite than I had been. She even sort of curtseyed. Where that came from I don't know. Maybe she'd seen it on television. "You're so pretty," Callie said, still staring.

"Why, thank you, Callie," BB said.

Nina touched BB's hand and said, "I hope you'll stay in town a few days. Tavy will come around. She's just needs a little time to adjust."

I realized that was probably true. It would be nice to have some hours alone to sort out my feelings. Which were whirling around inside of me like my stomach was doing laundry.

Before I could answer, Palmer entered the house, and a whole new set of introductions began. That kept us busy enough that no one noticed how near to tears I was. My mother and father had stayed together and *still* didn't get in touch with me. Maybe I hadn't noticed at the age of, say, a couple of months, that my parents rejected me, but it was now acutely clear. It's not as if I had never wondered where my real father and mother were. There were times when I felt angry or sad about their absence even though I loved Nina and Palmer, and loved them for adopting me. When I was a teenager I would Google my birth mother's name, Babette, but couldn't get far beyond *Babette's*

Feast, a movie I never saw based on a book I never read. I suppose I was regressing. In fact, I suppose I was being a bratty toddler all over again.

Our basement apartment consists of two small rooms, the laundry sink, and a half bath. We take baths on the second floor, across the hall from where Nina and Palmer sleep. Obviously, it's not ideal. Of our two rooms, one is my bedroom/studio and the other, originally the safe room where occupants would wait out tornadoes, is even smaller and serves as Callie's bedroom. Sometimes she'll be practicing in her room while I'm in mine, painting. That's a really good feeling but I can't assume it will always be enough for Callie or, truthfully, for me either.

Was I was wrong and Hollywood was not full of phonies? Maybe BB was a nice, normal person, as real as anyone else. Her jewelry was certainly real. The necklace and jade earrings, the bracelet cuff on her upper arm, snazzy simple watch on the left wrist. Nina later told me the watch was by Patek Philippe, whoever that is. (Me, I wear Timex.) The tee-shirt could have been from anywhere, but her designer jeans cost more than my entire wardrobe. Yet she didn't come across like someone dressed in money.

Still, for someone with a gentle demeanor, she's the center of the room. When she walks into the living room, it turns into a stage. The three-way floor lamp becomes a spotlight. She knows exactly where to stop, when to turn, when to speak. Without marks. I don't mean her actions are scripted, she just has an actor's instincts.

I calmed down somewhat, and we all went out for dinner and BB wound up staying in Madison. A couple of days later Nina suggested that I might want to paint BB. I knew Nina had an ulterior motive—to get us to spend time together—but then I thought, as if it were my own idea, *I should paint her*. How often did someone who looked like her come down the pike?

I've done portraits of Nina. A couple. They're sort of cubist. The painter who should have painted Nina was Braque. He'd have registered the planes and angles of her face. But when Nina sat for me, I couldn't get on canvas what I was seeing. She has a way of looking present and pleasant and interested while at the same time her eyes reveal that she's thinking about her writing. She once told me about riding in the car with her father when they lived in Virginia: he'd be driving according to the speed limit and then he would get slower and slower and slower, and Eleanor would turn to the back seat to announce that Art was working on the slow movement. Same thing when he speeded up: the allegro. Nina was like that: her thinking showed. I kind of hated her for it for a while. A daughter wants her mother to pay attention to her. A lot of the time Nina did, she did pay attention to me, but the rest of the time I had to do things to get her attention. I had to speak up for myself. I had to get pregnant and *keep the baby*. Well, not really. But anyone who has a writer for a mother feels the gaps when her mind is on her work.

Gaps and gaps. Sometimes I think all the things anyone does are done to get attention. Even if we don't recognize the dynamic in ourselves—we feel we don't need to be congratulated or pointed out or talked about—we still want to be loved.

I give myself a good talking-to before Nina has to do it. *Snap out of it*, I say to myself. *Suck it up*. I snap to it. I suck it up. I do what Nina wants me to do before she says it again. Besides, I've begun painting BB's portrait now. It was kind of strange at first. I know we both felt that, but painting is what I do, and in a way posing is what BB does.

In the morning three windows on the northwest wall and two on the southeast channel the light into the basement; then it begins to leave, but I have no trouble remembering BB's face in early afternoon.

We talk, admittedly somewhat stiffly at first. As Nina knew, I can't just stand here with a paintbrush in my hand while BB stands there looking back at me. Even with the music loud, it's awkward not to talk.

"How did you and Nina get along when you were pregnant with me?" I ask her. I have my paints out and she's standing beside my easel. Yes, I've invited her down here.

"Fine." She touches her face. I've noticed she does that a lot. Touches her eyebrows, her left cheek, her forehead. Sort of as if she is afraid her face is going to desert her.

Sometimes BB holds her face between her hands as if it is a word inside parentheses.

"What were you like at fourteen?" I ask.

"Oh, I don't know. I wanted to get away from my mother. Isn't that what every fourteen-year-old girl wants?"

"No," I said. "It wasn't what I wanted. My mom and I have always been friends."

"Mine didn't know what to do with me. She shipped me off to my aunt."

"What a bummer. Nina let me stay home. Well, that's not really accurate—she wouldn't have let me out of her sight."

"And you *kept the baby*. I know."

"Well, why didn't you? Keep me?"

"My mother couldn't afford two kids. There was the baby and there was also me. I was too young to get a job. And Nina wanted a baby. It was a win-win-win situation." Three *wins*.

"Nobody consults the baby. Move your chin back down, BB."

"Like this?"

"Perfect."

"I hitched to California with my boyfriend. It would have been a horrible life for you, one-room apartment, no pets. Sometimes we didn't eat."

"Didn't *eat*? That's a little hard to believe."

"Nevertheless. Sometimes someone would sneak Roy onto a construction crew. We picked grapes. Before he got jobs in the industry."

"So—did it occur to you that maybe I would wonder about my birth mother? Did you think that—I mean, you could have maybe called sometime, in twenty-six years."

"I thought it was better for you—and Nina—if I didn't."

"You vanished from the earth."

"We were selfish, Tavy. I don't know what else to say."

The bald statement brings me up short. I kind of admired her for admitting it. "When did you become BB?"

"It was Roy's nickname for me. He thought *Babette* was old-fashioned. He thought *BB* would pop on a marquee."

It pulled me up even shorter to realize we'd been talking nonstop. And she had questions, too—for example, why I chose painting. As if there was any choice about it. She talked about my grandfather's/uncle's painting. Apparently it was abstract. She asked me who Callie's father is and if I hear from him. She asked me if I wanted more kids and I said, "Not as long as I'm in the basement."

"We'd love to have you visit us in Malibu," she said. In almost the same breath, as if scared I might say no, she asked me about high school and prom and I told her I never much cared about either one. She asked me about college.

Then she asked me what had drawn me to Zayed. I don't think about him as obsessively as I used to, but now I stopped to think how to answer her question and what came to mind were his arms, his sleek, smooth, muscled, obsidian arms. What it was like being held by them. I found myself wondering who he's got them wrapped around now. Which is stupid, because I don't care. It's been years.

BB stayed for a week. There was so much estrogen in the house that I asked Palmer how he could stand it. "Nina's my second wife, as you know," he said. "You might not know that my first wife left me for a woman. I've been befogged by estrogen for years. By now I'm oblivious to it." He tousled my hair as if I were still a kid and went upstairs.

Then Roy showed up.

To be treated the way he treated her. He anticipated her every need, her every *wish*. He kept his arm around her, held her hand, read her face for clues.

I looked for myself in him but I wasn't there. "Roy," BB said, "here she is." He felt even bigger than he looked when he enclosed me in a hug. But who, exactly, was this guy, my body seemed to be saying as I backed out of his embrace, even though he was a dark-haired version of Brad Pitt. Then when BB said, "I hope we can persuade Tavy to visit us, maybe for a long time," he smiled.

When he sat down, he leaned forward in his seat, hunching, extravagantly expensive shirt and blue jeans and brown leather belt, the shoes no doubt custom made, watch that I'm sure could tell not only time but the barometric pressure in the Magellanic clouds, and smiled, and said nothing.

"Well, Roy, how does it feel to be the father of me?" I said.

He cleared his throat. His voice was slightly guttural. "It feels fine."

He looked at BB, as if asking if his response was satisfactory. BB said, "Roy wants to get to know you better, just as I do."

"I do," he said. "You're my daughter." He sighed, a long, deep sigh, and slid down on the seat, and his handsome face kind of collapsed. "We were shits," he mumbled. He straightened up again, this time leaning so far out of his seat that he might have fallen. "I—you must think we never thought of you, but we did. Do. Never stopped. We were just so young, we knew we were too young, we thought you would be better off with your great-aunt. I mean, she had a house and a job, we were practically homeless."

BB had her hands in her lap. They were clasped, as if she were praying. "Weren't you?" she asked.

"How can I compare what was with what might have been?" I said.

Nina said, "Sweetie, why don't you go to California for a week? Callie will be fine. We'll get her where she needs to be. It will be fun for me to have the time with Callie."

Callie tugged at my hand and said, "This is a dumb book."

And I said, not knowing I would say it, All right. Maybe because Roy and BB just looked so worried and hopeful. The shock of meeting them had worn off. For years, they'd been vague fantasies but now they were real, and BB no longer seemed so hard to talk to. I was now curious about them and wanted to know more. Plus, of course, it would be nice to escape the basement for a little while.

I thought I would wait until Callie was farther along in her school year. It was her first and I needed to be there until she was settled. But then I was painting and there was Thanksgiving and Christmas and Callie's first time trading valentines in school and somehow it was the next August before I flew to California.

The house surprised me with its smallness, but it was on the ocean and must have cost a fortune as it was. I guess you'd need another fortune to buy a bigger house by the Pacific. Huge glass windows framed the ocean in all its moods—slow and foggy, blue and bouncy, the surf so white it looked bleached. They put me in a room on what seemed like a mezzanine: the house was modern, with jutting and receding planes, and it wasn't always easy to know what floor you were on. I had a bed, a nightstand, a chair, a small table, dresser, lamp, and my own bathroom. There was also a vanity, which struck me as a very California thing.

The first morning, I wended my way downstairs—and there *was* wending—to find BB and Roy in the kitchen. "Good morning," I said.

"You too," BB said. Roy pushed his chair back and pulled one out for me. "Did you sleep well?" he asked.

"Sure," I said.

Roy handed me a cup of coffee. It was Jamaica Blue Mountain and tasted like heaven. BB put a plate of fruit and a bowl of cereal in front of me. I grabbed an apricot. "I don't know what you're expecting," I said.

"We're not expecting anything," they said, in unison. BB added, "You can do whatever you want. Sunbathe. Walk on the beach. Go shopping."

"Do you need spending money?" Roy asked, digging for the wallet in his back pocket. I observed that my father's stubble was artistically assembled. Yeah, I know hair grows where it grows and doesn't where it can't, but it *looked* planned. Or should I say *intended.*

"No, no," I said. "I don't want to go shopping. I think I'll check out the beach."

"There's sunscreen on the counter," BB offered. "Out here, you really need to slather it on."

In a flash I was out the house and following the path, apricot in hand, conversation—halting, awkward, strained—behind me.

After a day or two, the ocean had had its way with me, and I was calm, calmer than I'd been, it seemed, in my whole life—mellow, even. The sun was a massage therapist, and stress moved out of my body. This is what we miss in Wisconsin—we miss not having to fight the weather every step of the way. BB was relaxed and happy, too. Roy went to his office every day, but he was home by four-thirty, and we all had drinks on the patio before dinner. They had a cook but the meals were simple—fish and vegetables, gazpacho, omelets, salads (Cobb, Caesar, Niçoise). One night, just split-pea soup and bread, but it was amazing bread.

BB told me about the baby who died, and I got pretty choked up because I imagined how I would have felt if . . . I can't even say it. She surely thought I was upset about her loss, and I didn't want to say I wasn't, that I was on the verge of crying about something that had not even happened to me. And at the same time I *was* sorry about her loss. I'm so glad I'm not a writer. If I were a writer I'd have to try to make sense of this.

As we got closer over the days, BB grew more and more solicitous of me. She would tuck a blanket around me if we were in the living room and the night was chilly. If we were sitting side by side she'd play with my hair the way Nina used to, curling a strand around her finger or plaiting a single braid. She's taller than I am, which contributed to my adoration of her—yes, adoration. With honey-blonde hair and translucent emerald eyes, she looked like a fourteenth-century icon, a thing to be adored. I think I was in a kind of trance. Maybe I can blame it on the beach.

On the patio we clinked our glasses and toasted ourselves over and over. Venus hung low in the sky, the moon overblown at first and shrinking as it rose, the sound of the surf steady but not insistent, not begging, not clamoring, just—present. Without getting out of it, BB shuffled her chair over to mine and linked arms with me. Roy's face was pensive. I asked him what he was thinking.

"I'm a lucky man," he said.

"Because you're rich and famous?" We were getting close enough that I figured he could take my sarcasm as this natural part of me.

He snorted. (No, not cocaine, just a short laugh.) "I do okay but mostly nobody here is actually rich. A few people. The rest of us have big nuts."

I hoped he wasn't talking about his genitals.

"A nut is the sum of the debts you owe. The mortgage, the rented Cadillac, the lawyer, the housekeeper, the dry cleaner, what have you. As for fame—how many directors can you name, right now, off the top of your head? There are a lot of us out here, and most of us just aren't famous. Or they have fame for a month or two if the film is good but then it fades into thin air." He demonstrated fading by moving his hands away from each other.

"Then why are you lucky?"

"I'm lucky because I knew what I wanted. I wanted to make pictures. And then I met your mother and wanted to be with her. A lucky person is someone who knows what they want. Indecision strangles you. Or wears you out. Knowing what you want is a gift from the gods."

If that was the case, I had to admit that I was lucky too.

Roy reached across the table and punched me, not hard, on my arm. "We're lucky to have you back in our lives, kid."

I began to be glad that Roy was my birth-father. And of *course* he had not assembled his stubble. He was just lucky with that, too.

An unseen artist painted a cloud over the moon.

Each evening before drinks I Skype Callie. I tell her I love her. She tells me she loves me. I ask her what she did today. Did she play with her friends? Did she practice? Is she behaving? I ask these ordinary questions but what I really want to do is reach in and haul her out of the Internet and the computer screen onto my lap and hug her and hold her. She's so sweet. How can anybody be that sweet? She didn't get it from me, I know. She didn't get it from Zayed Mbawe, either. There must be a gene for sweetness that skipped a generation—or five or six or ten generations—and smuggled itself into Callie's DNA.

It stuns me to learn that BB is almost deaf in one ear. I find out when she's in the kitchen one morning. "Would you like some orange juice?" I ask her, as I'm pouring myself some. No answer. I ask again. Still no answer. I wonder if I somehow offended her last night. I set the container of orange juice by her elbow. She looks up. "Oh, Tavy," she says, "thanks for getting it out of the fridge. Would you like some?"

"Birth defect," she says when I ask. "I haven't put my hearing aid in yet."

"That must have been hard, growing up," I say.

"I'm used to it."

"Is that why you're so quiet?"

"Oh, I'm not so quiet," she says, but I know she is, and now I know that sometimes she misses what other people are saying. From here on, I make a point of facing her whenever I say anything.

The fourth day, BB and I went for a walk on the beach. She asked me what I think of Nina's books. I explain that when I was fourteen I asked Nina if I could read them. Nina was silent for a couple of minutes before she said, "You're free to read the books, of course. I can't and won't stop you from reading them. But I wish you wouldn't." I asked why. "It will make me self-conscious," she said, "and I might start censoring myself so you won't change your opinion of me." That made sense to me. I have some drawings—had some even back then—that I would never want her to see. So I promised her I wouldn't read her books. But when I came home from Evergreen, I asked her again, and she said okay.

"You can find the whole list online," I said to BB.

"What are your favorites?"

"The collected stories, I think. And *The Visitors*, a novel. The most recent book. She said it scared her to write that one."

BB wanted to know why.

"Lots of stuff about death in it," I said.

BB was picking up shells the whole time I was talking. Collecting shells seemed pointless to me, since you can buy them at stores. She said, "Nina must be driven."

"She's not," I said. "She just loves what she does. I'm the same way about painting."

"Still, hasn't she missed a lot of life?"

"I think she's probably lived more than most people because she lives with so many people—all the characters in her books."

"If acting were my entire life I'd kill myself."

"Why don't you do something else?" I asked.

"I am. I'm pregnant."

I stopped walking. So did she. We were facing each other on the beach. The pockets of her hoodie were pooched out from the sea shells that stuffed them. Pregnant. This was unexpected, to say the least. The breeze flipped her hair in front of her face and she pushed it back but as soon as she let it go it whipped around again.

"When?" I asked.

"When am I due? In seven months. Don't tell anyone. I shouldn't be telling you. It's early. There's no guaran—" The "tee" fell from the sentence like a shingle from a roof.

"It will be fine," I said. "Better than fine." I reached out to hug her. Over her shoulder I could see women in bikinis playing volleyball. We had been to art galleries, the pier, the farmers' market, where BB bought that great bread.

When you paint, or rather, when you've learned to see what's in front of you and you decide to paint it, the world rushes in on you. I imagine a newborn feels like this, inundated, confused, and frightened. Shapes, colors, composition, perspective fly toward you like a flock of birds. Instinct tells you to lower your face. You can feel like you're in that Hitchcock film, *The Birds*. You think your eyes are about to be stabbed and eaten, your face clawed, that you will die of suffocation by feathers. It's not easy just to stay standing and keep looking. And then you realize that what you thought was an assault has become an embrace; the painting-to-be surrounds you, and you are in a place of enormous possibility. This is what it is like to make art. Of any kind, I'm sure of that. I've seen Nina's face when she's in that place, her hair in disarray with or without a styling wand, her shirt half out of her jeans, her eyes unfocussed. We both live in that unnamed country where there's no borderline and no sign telling travelers which way to go.

I flew back to Madison.

I was eager to kiss Callie hello. We would go for a Happy Meal, which I didn't usually let her have. I would blow on her neck and make her giggle. I would sew the buttons missing from her coat back on long before winter arrived. I would hug her and hug her and hug her until she would never forget how much I love her.

I took the shuttle from the airport to the house. Callie ran into my arms and I did blow on her neck and hug her and kiss her.

"How do you catch a monkey?" she asked.

"I don't know," I said.

"You hang from a tree and make a noise like a banana!" She clapped her hands over her mouth, grinning. "I learned that at school," she said. Palmer came downstairs. I was expecting him to be at the university. He said he needed to talk with me. But first he spoke to Callie. "Callie," he said, "your grandmother wants you to come up." Callie was wearing a red corduroy jumper, green shirt, and blue Mary Janes. She raced upstairs.

Palmer's gaze followed Callie until she was gone. Then he turned and looked at me. Just looked. Plunged his hands into his pockets. Continued to look. "You're making me nervous," I said. "What's up?"

He combed his hair with his fingers, something I'd been watching him do since I was a child. There was less hair now, but still enough that it always looked uncombed. I almost offered to get out the styling wand for him.

"Sweetie," he said, "your mother's sick."

It was my turn to stare. "What do you mean, sick?"

"Sweetie, I have to tell you something first. Let's go sit down."

"You're scaring me."

I sat down right where I was, on the stairs. Palmer sat down beside me. He put his arm around me. "She's not going to get well."

The body tells us what we feel. I felt as if the room had tipped up and I was about to slide down.

"She's not going to die immediately," he said.

Palmer hadn't shaved and his stubble wasn't artistic or even assembled; it was just dull gray patches here and there, sort of as if he were growing mold. He looked as if he hadn't slept. How could I see these details when the rest of reality was slipping away?

My mouth was so arid I could barely speak and I began to tremble. Then I realized he hadn't told me what she had. "What is it?"

"Pancreatic cancer," he said.

This time the earth disappeared from under my feet, the stairs, the house. Palmer pulled me into his arms and I wept on his shoulder. He kissed me on my forehead and patted the top of my head.

Callie came skipping back down the stairs. "Grandmom's asleep," she said in her soft voice, and then, as we turned, she stopped mid-stride halfway down and raised her voice to a screech. "Mommy, what's wrong?" Without waiting for an answer she hurried down the rest of the way.

"Your grandmother's ill," Palmer said.

"Tell her the truth," I said. And to Callie I said: "Your grandmother is dying." I seized her by the waist and gathered her to me. The three of us on the same step. I looked at Callie and she blinked. Her eyes were huge in her small face. For a moment she said nothing. Then she said, burying her face in my neck so that her sweet, warm breath was on me, "Shiitake."

On the Care and Handling of Infants and Small Children

Children arrive on earth after a long voyage through space and time. They are greeted by light. The stage of development in which they arrive is the baby stage. The babies are at first dazed, then bedazzled, then dizzied as they are turned upside down and slapped into breathing, at least until recently. A baby always arrives on its birthday.

There are no secondhand babies; they are always new. Their skin is as new as tomorrow. Their eyes are so new that they shine like a new car. Their tiny hands open and close like clams. Their noses are small and cool, like seashells.

Rule #1: Don't handle, dandle!

So babies won't catch cold, they must be wrapped, in cloth or parental arms.

Babies have outlines for eyebrows but are still waiting for the color to be filled in.

Don't expect babies to know what to do with their arms and legs. They have to grow into them.

Babies have big heads and small bodies. If you sing to one it will likely fall asleep. If you squeeze it, the baby will cry. Do not squeeze the babies.

You may smell the baby. It has a delightful baby smell as long as its diaper is not full.

Be sure to chuck your baby under the chin. Babies like that.

Even if you do not squeeze the baby, it will sometimes cry. It may need a diaper change or a feeding, or a gentle hug. To stop babies from crying, cradle them, coo at them, and tell them they are loved. Like this: "We have been waiting for you, dear baby. We are so happy to welcome you."

Or maybe not. Maybe there is no family awaiting the baby, maybe the baby is unwanted.

What a sadness there is then. Light leaves the room. The world darkens. The baby is whisked away—to an orphanage, perhaps, where other unwanted babies may or may not be friendly to the newest one. Who has ever been friendly to them? Everyone wants a parent, preferably two. Everyone wants a little bit of love.

The ears of babies need stimulation. If you want your baby to be happy all its life, set it down in the middle of a string quartet. Let the baby crawl around the violinists' and the violist's feet. Even the cellist's feet if the cellist can play in tune. The music will soak into the baby; it will hear that music in its mind always. Even when the baby is grown up and sad, that music will play in its mind and the baby will smile.

Until babies learn to walk, they spend a lot of time in cradles and cribs. Make these fun places to be. Mobiles are good, as are soft toys of the right size. Throw in a rainbow or two and see how your baby's face lights up.

But clowns can scare very small babies.

As your baby grows, the body will catch up with the head, though not for several years. What big brains the little buggers have.

Oh baby. Oh baby, baby.

The Only News that Matters

Conrad looked up from his desk in the medical library to see Palmer Wright headed his way. He pulled up a chair and Palmer dropped into it as if he could not stand up for another second. As if the chair brought him not only physical but emotional support.

Beneath the dim fluorescent lighting—years ago the university removed one light bulb from every overhead fixture to save on costs—Palmer's face looked blank and tired.

Conrad and Palmer were neighbors, and had been for a couple of decades, though their encounters were limited to block parties or the occasional drink with their respective spouses.

"Hey, Conrad, so this is where you work. Maybe you can point me in the right direction?"

"I'll do my best. What do you need?"

Palmer looked in his breast pocket as if that was really where he needed to be. He came up with a pen as he said, "Uhhh, I'm looking for information on pancreatic cancer."

They really didn't know each other very well, and now here was this huge undisclosed, invisible but palpable package between them, on Conrad's desk. A package that said "to" followed by the name of the person with pancreatic cancer, but the label was blurred.

"Do you want surgical information?"

"Not really. More like—prognosis, pain, consciousness."

"Of course," Conrad said. "Have a seat and I'll take a look around."

In the reading room, Palmer was surprised—if only for a moment—to find the medical library like any other library. He realized he'd been imagining an anatomical museum. This was indeed a library, with long tables, chairs, lamps, and walls lined with books.

Conrad wasn't sure whether he should tell his wife about Palmer's visit. When he let himself into his house, Quinn was already home. She had started a fire in the fireplace and as he sat down in the armchair she handed him a drink. Madison was a wine-and-cheese city, but he felt far enough removed from the academics to indulge in a nightly whisky or g-t. He could scarcely believe that this was his life now. With repainted walls and changed furniture, he had nearly as much trouble remembering that this was the same house he had lived in with his first wife. Not that he wanted to remember—the deaths of his first wife and son were, he wanted to believe, tried hard to believe, the memories of a younger man, a man who no longer existed because if he did he would have to kill himself to escape the pain of his grief. The Conrad of today was married to Quinn, a secretary for the History Department, though not a personal secretary to Palmer; the university wouldn't fork up money for personal secretaries for faculty. Especially since the advent of computers, faculty were their own secretaries. Conrad and Quinn had two boys, both older than his son was when—. Well, *when*. They were thirteen and ten, boys who knew virtually nothing about their father's former life. One was good at mechanical things, the other at mathematics. Both were swimmers, with long torsos and capacious lungs, and Scouts. There was no sibling rivalry; they got along with each other.

Drinking his drink in front of the fire, Conrad let his eyes rest on the view from the window. The days were growing shorter, but trees still bore leaves. The leaves were aflame, maples burning red, poplar agleam with golden lights. The blue spruce did look somewhat bluish. But just as he and his neighbors were aging, so was the neighborhood. Neatly sectioned flower gardens had grown shaggy, had subdivided and encroached and overrun. Trees were taller and thicker. Once-pint-sized maple volunteers were thirty years bigger.

Quinn sat down across from him and raised a glass of her own. "Cheers," she said.

Quinn was compact and curvy. Her khaki-colored hair fell halfway down her back in a cascade of curls. Conrad often wondered what she could possibly see in him.

Firelight fell on Conrad's face so that he appeared to be blushing.

They had not yet had a snowfall. The day had been gusty and leaves, loosened, flying from branches, soared and turned before they fell, traveling in flocks. The wind blew the clouds away, too, leaving behind a clear blue sky so glasslike it might have been a mirror. A mirror in which a quiet medical librarian might see himself as a man of some profundity even though he chose not to act on what he believed. Because he might be a Wisconsin progressive but he was also a husband and father and in his experience protecting one's family was more important than saving one's country from itself. Did his family know how much they needed his protection? Probably not, but *he* knew—he knew exactly how fragile and tentative were their lives, their beings, and it was to them he owed his deepest allegiance.

A man who has lost his wife and son in an automobile accident is obliged to not remember the past, for if he does, he will be lost in it forever, paralyzed by grief. A man who has lost his wife and son must find a new life or die in the old one. Nor may he allow himself to think about the old one in regard to the new one or he will go mad trying to protect his new sons, his new wife. And they—the new wife, the new sons—would rebel against that—of course they would, anyone would. The only solution was to keep his mind on other things: for example, that God died in the trenches of World War One, but religion has lingered for another century. It, too, is now dying, and terrorism is the long, last gasp of religious fundamentalism, dinosaur trapped in a tar pit. And that corporate greed will ultimately consume itself (but maybe not before it destroys freedom). That a planet without polar bears or honeybees or snow leopards might also become a planet without polar caps or wildflowers or wildlands. There were certainly plenty of things to worry about. The START Treaty, the Tea Party, Sumatra, drug cartels in Mexico, lead in Chinese toys, the homeless in America. Putin's vendetta against Khodorkovsky in Russia, the ridiculous cost of health care in a country (ours) with one of the highest rates of infant deaths—and wasn't that a helluva paradox?

Conrad liked to say of himself that he'd "always been a current events addict." He read about regimes and republics, dictators and anarchists, economic meltdowns, natural disasters, and environmental waste. He watched CNN and MSNBC and read the *New York Times* online. He was convinced that America was sliding into authoritarianism, an oligarchy of massive corporations that, because they owned information about everyone, would be able to control everyone. It was rule by Big Brother but this time Big Brother was incomprehensibly rich—rich with bucks and data. The survivalists had gotten it all wrong; the way things were now, nobody could opt out. Everybody was a consumer, with habits, preferences, desires, needs, nothing secret, nothing private. We were all on the map, and the map was in Big Brother's hands.

Especially in Wisconsin, which had made a sharp turn to the right. The local news was as alarming as the global news.

Conrad's round face, with its circumflex moustache over the O of his mouth, was reminiscent of an earlier era. He might have been a butler or bank president in nineteenth-century England. Instead he was subject liaison in a library in the twenty-first infuriating century. Infuriating because the greedy rich got greedier and richer while the ranks of the poor swelled. Infuriating because terrorists held freedom hostage. Infuriating because neglect and misuse were depleting the planet of resources. Conrad was passionate about his politics and if, as surely all could agree, the twentieth century was a nightmare, then the twenty-first, in his opinion, was a wakeup call. Yet people, he thought—thought with amazement—were sleepwalking through their lives.

But he could not be the one to tell them that, for he was a modest man, unassuming and diligent, and he hated confrontations.

He wasn't a wacko, just a man with more intellectual energy than his job required, who had put his old life far behind him precisely by virtue of thinking about other things, such as the pretty pass America had come to. He didn't rail at friends or harass his wife with his ideas, and if his ideas were insane, which he did not for one moment believe, they kept *him* sane by keeping him occupied. Life was chockfull of paradoxes like that. You either accepted them or went way, way, way around the bend.

He was alive and blessed. As long as he lived in the present.

He remembered that when he was growing up there had been time for everything: archery at camp, pick-up games of basketball, hours of reading whatever he wanted to read, not just schoolbooks. Nor was this freedom peculiar to kids: he remembered his mother taking time out of her morning to drink coffee and chat with her friends. He and his parents used to pile into the car and go for drives on Sunday afternoons. He remembered his parents sitting on the front porch in the evening, his dad whispering into his mother's ear, her girlish giggling, the way she clapped her hands when somebody said something amusing. No, something had happened to time, not simply to his perception of it. Everyone worked longer for less, mere information-gathering chopped up the day, and even his sons' schedules intruded and kept them away from him.

He bought a pricey notebook in which he kept a log, recording notable events. He never thought of it as a diary because he avoided the personal in it, but now and again the personal intruded anyway. On the first page he had written in script *The Private Notebooks of Conrad Tisch*, feeling confident that the notebooks would be plural. There was never an end to the news, local, national, global, or from outer space. His paragraphs aped the "Findings" section in *Harper's Magazine*. Thus he'd written:

> 2009. *January*. Obama and Biden sworn in. *February*. Health Care and deficits. Stimulus plan. Traveling from the very edge of the solar system, a green comet whizzed by the planet. It's the cyanogen gas that makes it look green. Scientists say our brains have a "love circuit." There's actually a particular spot linked to poor suckers who were wildly in love but have been dumped. Another connects to people who've been together a long time. The Ventral pallidum registers attachment, defined by the article I read as "people madly in love after twenty years." And of course, one spot is specifically for new love. They found this out by studying a species of monogamous rodent, i.e., the prairie vole. Dopamine plays a role. So losing a partner means going through withdrawal from addiction. One scientist says it's similar to "craving cocaine." Tell me about it. *May*. California Supreme Court declines to strike down ban on gay marriage. Jesus, California, have a heart. *June*. Air France 447 vanishes off the coast of Brazil. How many husbands will have lost their wives, I wonder. *July*. Palin resigns as governor of Alaska. Now if she would just resign from our television set. *September*. The city council has declared the plastic pink flamingo Madison's official bird. In 1979 students planted Bascom Hill in 1,008 plastic pink flamingos. I wasn't here for that, but the image is still everywhere, on postcards and so forth. *December*. The underwear bomber. On Christmas Eve, for godsake.
>
> 2010. *January*. Patdowns introduced at airports. Huge earthquake in Haiti. If there's any place that didn't need an earthquake, it's Haiti. Runaway unemployment. This comes on top of last year's bank

failures and bailouts. Thanks to all the hedge fund managers. *February.* A biology professor at the University of Alabama in Huntsville goes on a shooting rampage and kills three faculty members and wounds three others. Seems she was unhappy about not getting tenure. If that's all it takes, the Madison faculty should live in fear. *April.* Volcano in Iceland explodes. The ash plume is causing havoc for travelers, stranding planes at airports. BP oil spill. All those lovely aquatic creatures killed. All those people killed. BP hems and haws. Our Tea Party ideologue candidate Scott Walker suggests eliminating seniors and family from health care coverage. He says he's got the state's best interests at heart. Sure. Get rid of the old and the young, tax the hell out of the middle class, and turn Wisconsin into a haven for corporate crooks. A meteor falls on Wisconsin. By which I mean a meteor, not that dumb-as-a-piece-of-coal Walker. *September.* Over 14.3 percent of Americans are living in poverty. How can we tolerate this? How can we pretend we are a civilization and not just a holding pen for poor people? *November.* Tom DeLay's financial finagling has caught up with him. I'm happy to say! *December.* Julian Assange, the guy in charge of WikiLeaks, has been arrested in England. Ostensibly for sexual assault, but probably for performing the public function of providing citizens with information unlawfully withheld from them.

2011. *January.* Floods in Australia. *February.* Mubarak ousted from power in Egypt. Democrats have hied themselves to Chicago so there could not be a quorum in the state legislature. Take *that*, Scott Walker! *March.* Earthquake and tsunami in northern Japan cause meltdowns at several nuclear reactors. Radioactive cesium-137 roughly equal to 168 Hiroshimas, but this is slow, and Hiroshima was lightning fast. Not that that is a lot of comfort. Elderly Japanese have volunteered to work to contain leakage. *May.* Berlusconi bunga-bungas while Italy sinks deeper in debt. Navy Seals take out Osama bin Laden. *July.* Famine in Africa. Drought in Africa. Children

> dying in Africa. Crazed right-winger goes on killing spree in Norway. *August.* Debt crisis in Europe. Greece, Spain, Portugal, Italy, Ireland, England. Recall elections salvage two Senate seats for Democrats in Wisconsin. That's not enough, but it's something. Ali Ferzat, a well-known Syrian political cartoonist, is kidnapped, beaten, and left bleeding on the side of the road. Blame attaches to Syrian president Bashar al-Assad's security forces. Madisonians had marched on State Street in spring to protest the paycuts Walker mandated for state workers. We workers would like to see corporations pay their fair share. The only rich person who's willing to do that is Warren Buffett, and he doesn't live here. Walker says the paycuts will be made up for by not having to pay union dues. I guess he thinks he's a comedian. Muammar Gaddaffi on the ropes. Good riddance. Black hole swallows star and someone gets it on film. Prime Minister of Japan resigns. I hope he does not feel he has to commit hara-kiri. Scientists think they've found a planet made of diamond. I wish I could give it to my wife.

When Conrad flipped through his pages from beginning to end, he felt as if he had run a marathon and understood why he always felt pressured. There was too much news. Even in his edited version, there was too much news. It was a way of staying present, yes, but it was a present that pushed you around. A tense present. How had he never noticed this before?

He made a silent resolution to watch, read, or listen to the news less often. He would buy a novel and read it. He would spend more time listening to Mozart and Haydn. He would turn off, opt out, and unplug.

He would take Quinn to hear the Pro Arte at the Chazen. He would throw a football in the yard with the kids.

But five minutes later he wanted to turn the news back on. He rose from his chair and carried the remote across the room to Quinn. "I want you to keep control of this," he said.

She looked up and blinked. Her face shone in the midst of her voluminous hair.

"Are you sure?"

"Yes."

She rose in her turn and took the remote with her.

"Where is it?" he asked when she got back.

"I'll never tell."

There was still the computer. But when he returned from work the next day, the computer was gone. "You didn't!" he said.

"I did," she said.

He clamped his jaw shut to keep from complaining further.

The radio was gone, too. No more NPR.

He didn't develop tremors but in every other way it felt like withdrawal. What was worse was that the past began to encroach. He remembered keeping house as a widower, the cleaning, the maintenance, the meals for one. Soup and Saltines. Yogurt. McDonald's. The house had been silent but not altogether: now and again, a whisper of the past would roam the rooms as if searching for a place to settle.

Despite himself, he remembered his first wife. He slipped away to the men's room, keeping his head down, and when he got there he locked himself into a stall.

He remembered the day he and his first wife moved into the house. Her excitement, his pride. The baby on the way.

He remembered his first son and his legs felt as if some essential support had been snatched from him. He sat on the closed toilet lid. He wanted to bawl his head off. He felt like a child. He wanted his mother. His mother? What the hell was wrong with him? His parents had been dead for decades.

He stayed in the stall until he felt he had himself under control.

He washed his face in the sink before he went back to his desk. The phone rang. He picked it up and said, in a strangled voice, "Medical library."

It was Quinn, calling from the History Department. "Are you all right? You don't sound so good," she said.

He cleared his throat.

"I'm fine," he said.

"Honey, I'm feeling bad about not letting you hear the news. Do you really want to go through with this? You could just cut back. You don't have to go cold turkey."

"I do. I do have to go cold turkey," he said.

There was a moment of suspension. "All right," she said. "It's your decision. See you later, sweetie." She hung up.

It was all he could do to face the succession of days. He tried to focus on Quinn, but she was busy with her job and the kids. He tried to focus on the kids, but they were happy throwing the football to each other.

A man is a mystery to himself. He thinks he understands his decisions, obligations, place in society; he thinks he has a grip on himself. Then one day he starts ruminating. And realizes that in fact he knows nothing—nothing about himself or anyone else. What does he know about the older boy, for example? Does he have a girlfriend? Is he having sex? Surely not, at thirteen? Is he aware that women are people? Does he have a dream for his future?

And the younger, who sometimes surprises with his social acumen—at the age of ten. Does he enjoy school? Does anyone bully him? How much does he know about sex? What is his favorite book?

Conrad accepts that he is at a loss. So many current events, so little comprehension of the self. He tries to catch up. With his sons he starts chats that quickly peter out. One afternoon he goes home early and cooks dinner so Quinn won't have to; she tries to make it seem like a big deal, but it's clear it hasn't made that much difference to her.

One day he goes to the History Department to pick his wife up for lunch and finds Palmer Wright standing beside her. Conrad is surprised because he knows that Palmer spends most of his time at the Institute for Research, which is in a different building. He holds out his hand to Palmer, and Palmer shakes it.

"We're headed for lunch," Quinn says to Palmer. "Why don't you join us?"

Palmer hesitates, waving his arms around as he is apt to do.

"Please," says Conrad. Together they leave the sterile building, which, however, has a great view of the lake, and head to lunch.

After they order, Conrad asks Palmer "how it's going."

"Nina has pancreatic cancer," he says. For a moment, Conrad and Quinn, not knowing how to respond, freeze, become a painting on a wall. Then Quinn knocks her fork off the napkin and the clatter when it hits the floor seems to all three to call too much attention to their table.

"I was worried," Conrad confesses. "When you came into the library."

Quinn looks closely at her husband. Why didn't he tell her this?

Palmer combs his hair with his hands, a lifelong habit. He wants to make everyone feel better, wants to make himself feel better, wants most of all to make his absent wife feel better, but how? "She will be with us for a while yet."

The pizza has arrived, which gives Conrad and Quinn something to do with their jaws besides let them gape. Quinn puts a piece of pizza on Palmer's plate.

"Yes," Palmer says. "So there's no need to be gloomy just yet."

Maybe not, but Conrad looks at Palmer and sees the gloom lurking beneath his excitable face. It's in his brown eyes and the sagging bags beneath them. Son of a bitch, he thinks, even the well-known Professor Palmer Wright will now discover what it is to lose a wife. He'd somehow thought of Palmer as above the fray, protected against the slings and arrows of outrageous fortune. He can't help feeling a sympathetic sorrow for the man across from him.

"Not all pancreatic cancers are the same," Palmer continues. "And there are new treatments."

Conrad believes Palmer is fooling himself. But what else can the guy do?

They finish lunch. Leaving the restaurant, Palmer says to Quinn that he'll see her later; he wants to buy some zinc for Nina before he goes back to the office; there's a theory that zinc might help.

They watch him walk off.

"I'll see you at home."

Conrad turns toward Quinn. "Yep," he says.

When he arrives home a little after five—it's only a short walk from the medical library to his house—Quinn says, "Why didn't you tell me before? About Nina."

"There was nothing to tell. I didn't know it was Nina."

"You knew something. I could tell."

"He came into the library for info about pancreatic cancer. I had no idea it was his wife."

"I don't imagine *pancreatic cancer* was a term used in the Middle Ages."

"Me either. But what does it matter that I didn't say anything to you?"

She splutters and her khaki curls somehow get curlier. "Conrad, she's a neighbor! This is important news. You should have told me. I should have been to see her by now."

"News? This is not *news*."

"It's the only news that matters," she says. "The *only* news."

Conrad locates the television in the hallway closet, at the bottom, behind long coats and raincoats and the boys' baseball bats. He sets it up in the den and turns it on. It is a Saturday, and on the book channel host and author are discussing a book about frozen methane in eastern Siberia. Permafrost beneath the East Siberian Arctic Shelf is thawing as temperatures warm. The author says that the methane is leaking into seawater and the atmosphere. "This can trigger sudden and massive global warning," he says, and because the shelf is shallow the methane hasn't time to oxidize before it gets to the surface. The result is ever more methane in the atmosphere and offshore. Feedback will speed the process. Humanity will survive, but not in large enough numbers to maintain civilization.

The host points out that there is also the Snowball Earth hypothesis, the pandemic possibility, the likelihood of nuclear war followed by nuclear winter, and the population problem. Humanity might run out of fresh water. Or run into an agricultural crisis. A megatsunami. A new ice age. The supervolcano at Yellowstone erupted some 640,000 years ago and might again. Artificial intelligence could backfire, the artificially intelligent deciding that humans are intellectually deficient. Jocularly, he says, "It's hard to choose from all these scenarios."

The author ignores the host's good will. "All those other possibilities are redundant," he says. "The one that's going to happen by the end of this century will be caused by the leakage of methane gas."

The host briefly looks befuddled. How can he spin this for his audience? He decides to brazen it out. He faces the camera. "There you have it," he says. "Join us next week."

Conrad is thinking about the author's prophecy of doom. Maybe the author was wrong. He hopes so, for the sake of his kids.

Just as he thinks this, the thirteen-year-old comes into the room and flops down on the leather couch. "Dad," he says.

For once his son has sought him out. Conrad feels a swelling in his chest. He wishes the boys would seek him out more often.

"What's up?" Conrad asks.

"Slow day. Kinda bored."

"Boredom is the result of laziness."

"Yeah. I've heard you say that." The boy drawls the retort. Still, it's more than his son usually says to him. And he's still on the couch. And, Conrad thinks, it was an almost bullying thing to have said. "Do you want to throw the old football around a while?" Conrad asks.

"Not really."

Conrad feels rebuffed.

"You know, Dad, I've been thinking. I'm thirteen and I don't really know much about your life. I mean, before you married Mom."

"There's not much to know."

His son stares at him. Finally he says, "Dad, you had a whole life before you met Mom. That's not nothing."

"What do you want to know?" Conrad asks.

"I want to know more about *you*."

"Your mother and I were married on—"

"I know that, but you were married before."

Conrad clears his throat. "Yes."

"Who was she? What was she like?"

"She—she—"

"What?"

"She was sweet."

"Sweet?" He sees that his son expects more. But the more is horrible. The more is what he has been trying to keep out of his mind. Then sure enough, his son says, "There must be something else you can tell me."

"She was killed in a car accident."

"Omigod, Dad. Were you driving?"

"No. She was going for ice cream, with our son."

The boy sits up. "You had a son before me?"

Conrad croaks out a *yes*. The tears that were so close the other day come back to his eyes. Feeling claustrophobic, he takes an enormous breath, and breathing opens something up in him and thirty years of tears fall.

"Hey, Dad, please stop crying. Jesus, Dad, don't cry."

Conrad has no answer.

"Mom," his son yells. "Dad needs you! We're in the den!"

Quinn comes into the den and sees her husband sobbing uncontrollably.

"It's okay," Conrad says when he can get the words out. "I'm okay."

"We were just talking, Mom." He tries to comfort his father by patting him on the shoulder but it feels too awkward to do it for long and he lets his arm hang at his side.

"He's okay," Quinn tells her son, "but you should go upstairs."

The boy leaves and Quinn wets the towel at the bar sink and touches the corner of it to Conrad's forehead and face. Conrad says, "I didn't mean—I mean, I think I've been sort of absent all these years, but I didn't want—"

"Shh, shh, no, honey, distant, sometimes, yes, maybe."

"I loved her."

"I know. And there's nothing wrong with that."

"I felt like there was."

"Only because you thought you were hiding your feelings from me. But you weren't, you know. I always knew. A wife always knows. Everything is going to be all right now."

All right?

He thinks about methane, about wives who die, about what Scott Walker is doing to Wisconsin, this state he loves, about children starving in Sudan. But at the same time he feels, for the first time since forever, that he is home, that this is his home, he is here. "Shh," Quinn says, holding the damp towel to his forehead as if he is ill, as if he has a fever and needs the cooling cloth. She says it again.

The Dead Brother

Nina's brother has now been dead for over a quarter of a century but he still takes up space in her mind. She deliberately thinks of him as her *dead brother* in an attempt to remind herself that the ghost in her mind is not the real guy. She figures the real guy was probably more complicated than she understood—maybe—but he is dead and she has her own life to tend to. The dead brother's organs were parsed by medical students. The dead brother died when his daughter, Babette, was fourteen. The dead brother never knew *her* daughter, Tavy, nor Tavy's daughter, Callie. The dead brother never knew Palmer, and that's a good thing, considering that he did his best to destroy her first marriage. Which would have ended anyway, but still. The dead brother was not around when their parents died. The dead brother was not around for 9/11, Iraq, or Afghanistan. The dead brother has not read the books she has written since his death and if he had he would have made some sarcastic comment. Which she would have ignored. The dead brother sometimes whispers to her at night after Palmer is asleep. Sometimes she can feel his breath in her ear and it makes her nervous so she turns over on her side to be closer to Palmer. Usually the dead brother says something like, *There are no great female philosophers, no great female composers, and great female writers are an aberration*. Sometimes the dead brother asks, *What is the point of writing poetry in forms?* She replies, *They give me pleasure.* He says, *Women. You're all masochists. You want to be chained and controlled*, and she wonders what planet he lives on. Sometimes the dead brother accuses her of being driven. Of being bitter and driven. Of being angry, bitter, and driven. She knows there was a time when that was true, but it was long ago. Happiness swept over her like morning light and she pinned it down and hugged it close and has never let go. The dead brother insists that, although he was a dipsomaniac, he was never an alcoholic. This very fine distinction is over her head, especially as she can't make it jibe with the vodka he gulped before breakfast. Sometimes he would pour the vodka into an empty beer can, a not very good disguise. He tells her that in her crib she made up a song and sang it whenever anyone showed her a Haydn score and that is so sweet she's bewildered. How can he be so sweet and so mean? The dead brother is so alive to her that once in a while she forgets and thinks he is alive and then has to remind herself that he is her dead brother. Occasionally the dead brother will turn up in her study with his classical guitar and play a little Bach or Boccherini. He will tell her that his favorite question is *how*. She will tell him that her favorite question is *why*. He will look at her pityingly and say, *I know.* She reminds herself that he doesn't know everything. For example, he does not know how interesting the question *why* can be.

The dead brother will set his classical guitar aside and walk over to stand behind her as she writes by hand or types. If she's writing prose he'll say, *If you want to write a novel, you really need to confront God.*

You don't believe in God.

That's beside the point. You have to cross the ocean in a sailboat. Go to war. Work on high steel.

He worked on high steel.

You mean I need to be a man.

You said it, I didn't.

He believed one had to experience radical alone-ness. One had to test oneself. One had to put up a fight. In this, he was like many male novelists in the fifties and sixties but perhaps he didn't know that times had changed.

The dead brother plays a snatch of "Malagueña." She's afraid he will wake the house, although apparently no one else can hear him. *It's time for you to leave*, she says.

He blows her a kiss and leaves her alone with the story she's working on.

What is a story? A sentence leads to more sentences. There is a beginning, a middle, and an end. Or maybe not. Maybe there is only a beginning and a middle.

Faith, Hope, and Clarity

For much of her life Nina Bryant believed that kindness is the primary consideration in almost everything. That kindness is the First Law. That kindness could save the world from itself.

"O Love, O Charite!" wrote Geoffrey Chaucer. Loving-kindness, according to the Talmud. For Nina, being kind was the first step toward becoming, as she put it, human. But she had not always been kind.

She knew that there were in her pockets of despair, envy, fear, and confusion and that these had led her on occasion to be angry, bitter, and mean, emotions she had named The Uglies, as if they were the three Fates of Greek mythology. She wanted so much to be kind. And generous. Alas, behaving kindly toward someone—and she didn't always—did not mean she *was* kind. The praxis of kindness was necessary but not sufficient.

Charity itself had limits. One day, Nina, idling at her desk, wrote *charity* on a Post-It. It startled her with its closeness to *clarity*. What if Paul, in First Corinthians, had meant to write faith, hope, and *clarity*? A slip of the stylus could change everything.

Okay, he wasn't writing in English, but still. It was still worth thinking about.

Nina's life now, in her later years, was a struggle against pain and a failing effort to stay sensorially in touch with the world outside herself. She had cataracts. Her hearing grew worse each day; Palmer and Tavy had to shout at her. She could not detect or identify odors: gazpacho, fish, an egg—no difference. Pesto, at least that bought in a jar at the grocery store, smelled like nothing, or, more accurately, glue. Gorilla Glue. Which was now available in a smaller, monkey-size tube. Perhaps she wouldn't have felt so estranged from the world were it not for her illness; she was only sixty-eight. But because of her illness, she lived too much of the day in her mind, blurring the texture of life with a daydream. She could use a laptop for an hour or two a day, but it took all her strength and wore her out even though she used it in bed or on the couch downstairs. Nina's thoughts and feelings mingled with day-long dreams and at times it was hard to distinguish them.

She had planned to have a Great Late Age—a decade or two in which she would finish writing the books she had in mind to write—and she felt cheated, as if someone, anyone, had promised her more years. Could she blame God? No, she didn't believe in Him. Or Her. The real movers behind the universe were chance and circumstance. Mr. Chance and Mrs.—or should she say Ms?—Circumstance, that ageless couple.

Snow had arrived in Madison. Nina knew the lakes would freeze over, the Capitol night lights shining across Lake Mendota like a lighthouse. A beacon of justice. But maybe not justice, she thought. Maybe a budget bent out of shape by logrolling legislators. Maybe a debate never to be resolved, for that was how Wisconsin was: attractive but surprisingly cautious.

From her bedroom window she could see snow falling on the blue spruce. It was starting to cover the sidewalk. The otherworldly silence of snow settled on the house and street. Nina crept downstairs to make a cup of hot chocolate for Callie, who would be home any minute. Nina got out Callie's favorite mug, which showed a teddy bear playing a violin. She opened a bag of marshmallows and extracted one, then put back the bag. Briefly, she sat at the table, breathing hard. Her stomach hurt. From her kitchen window she saw the bare limbs of the lilac pulling on long gloves of snow. Then she heard her daughter and granddaughter clambering up the steps, unlocking the door.

Cocoa!" Callie cried when Nina handed her the cup, the marshmallow a tiny iceberg. Nina took the violin case from Callie and put it on the couch.

"Shouldn't you be in bed?" Tavy asked.

"Tired of sleeping," Nina said.

"But it's good for you."

"No, it's not. It is not at all good for me."

Tavy opened her mouth and closed it again. She was not going to argue with her mother. If her mother wanted to go outside and make snow angels in the snow, she still wouldn't argue with her mother. Her mother had earned the right to do anything she wanted.

Callie set down her mug. She had a chocolate moustache, which she tried to lick off with her tongue but she couldn't reach all of it. She wrapped her chilled hands around the mug.

"Did you have a good lesson?" Nina asked.

Callie bobbed her head up and down. "I played Bach."

"First Sonata in G minor," Tavy said.

Nina remembered that her father used to warm up on the Bach Chaconne.

Tavy and Callie had left their boots on the floor when they came in and were in their socks. They had tossed their coats, hats, gloves, and scarves on the living room couch. These items were damp with melting snow. The couch was now damp. Tavy saw her mother struggling to hang their things in the hall closet and took over.

Callie watched her mother removing their things from the couch and carrying them to the closet. Mothers seemed always to know where things went, while Callie knew she could stand in the middle of the house, book or toy in hand, and look all around and not know where to put it, that particular book, that particular toy. Often she heard music in her head, which distracted her. She would stop to listen to it. Did she hear voices, too? her grandmother asked her, but no, just music, and it might have been music she had heard previously or it might have been music she had made up: it was hard to tell which.

They sat on the couch. The living room was prematurely dark with snow clouds outside. Nina wanted to know where life might take her daughter and granddaughter after she was gone. She wanted to know their narratives, their storylines. "Do you think you'll marry when you grow up, Callie?" she asked. "Will you go to your high school prom?"

"What's a prom?" Callie was a small declension between Nina and Tavy.

"A dance. One where a boy asks you to dance with him."

"I don't know," Callie said. "Maybe no one will ask me."

"You'll be asked," Nina said. "I promise."

"I'm going to get married and have ten babies and teach them how to play the violin."

Nina envisioned ten babies, round-faced, gurgling, and smiling, sitting in the front row of an auditorium. As soon as she saw the picture in her mind she realized how happy it made her. Ten babies sitting and applauding. Ten babies standing, if wobbly, and drawing their bows across the strings. Ten babies with bright eyes and with music in their heads.

Callie slurped the last sip of her cocoa. Tavy carried the mug to the sink. Nina said, "Ten is a lot. Maybe you'll settle for one or two."

"Maybe," Callie agreed. "But probably not."

"Where will you live?"

"Here."

"Ten babies in the basement! That will be quite a crowd."

"They'll be good babies. They won't cry, unless I forget to feed them. I might forget sometimes."

"That would certainly make them cry."

"I'll make it up to them. I'll buy them computers."

"Computers!?"

"Yes, and they'll be so pleased."

"Indeed."

"And the computers will teach them how to write music."

"Oho! Is that what you want for Christmas? A computer with a music program?"

Callie threw her arms around Nina. "Thank you," she said.

Nina ordered, online, a computer for Callie's very own and a music notation program called Sibelius First, made by a company called Avid. Not even Beethoven could have stopped technological progress.

In the bedroom at night, stretched out on the bed, she and Palmer held hands. Nina loved how, after a little while, she could no longer differentiate her hand from his. The heat of both hands radiated through their bodies.

Bodies, Nina thought, were how human beings collect data—eyes, ears, nose, mouth, and skin—with which to survive. And propagate. She hoped Palmer would remember hers as it had been before she got sick. *If a body meet a body.* But as for data, there were now so many machines so efficient at data collection that a body was not always necessary, not even for propagation. She imagined a future race of robots who understood how to make more robots. It wouldn't be as much fun as sex but it would be more efficient. She called this Nina's Theory of Transubstantiation.

Palmer turned toward her on his side, and placed his right hand on her forehead. She found this oddly reassuring, as if he were reminding her that she still existed. She had been lucky, lucky, lucky to find Palmer. Without him, The Uglies would have eaten her alive. That's what those emotions or traits were—predators. Opportunistic diseases. She was dying, but it was better than dying from anger or bitterness or meanness.

"Penny," he said.

"I was thinking how lucky I've been."

"Me too," he said.

"I hope you'll get married again."

"I won't need to. Being married to you has convinced me I exist." After his first marriage, Palmer had felt ontologically insecure.

"But I want you to. Someone not too young but not too old, either. Around forty. She should be easy to get along with and outgoing, so she'll entertain and make sure you have friends. She should be slender but not gaunt, so she can gain a little weight when she needs it to keep her face from sinking inward. Get someone who doesn't color her hair; it's cheaper."

"You've given this some thought, I see."

"I have. If she has children of her own, of any age, make sure they play well together."

"Will do," he said.

"And never, *never* call her *sugar foot*."

"Why not?"

"I won't be your only wife, but I am your only sugar foot."

He kissed her hard on the mouth.

Lying in bed, Nina reviewed her so-called career. She called it so-called because, to her, writing was not a career; it was a calling. On the bookshelf across the room she could read the titles on her books' spines. *Southern Streets at Noon*, short stories about families in the South, especially the kids. Some of it based on her own childhood and adolescence in Virginia, some of it based on her mother's childhood in Louisiana and adolescence in Mississippi. *The Absolute,* a novel, also set in the South but about a composer. More almost-autobiography, but then again, not. *We Are Not Deceived in Our Impressions,* another novel, this time about theology and theologians. Emphatically not autobiographical. *Desperate Measures.* Stories about people who are forced to take them. She regretted the title; it had been used so often. *Dancing with Ava Martel,* a novel that reinvented Ford Madox Ford's novel *The Good Soldier.* Set in Hollywood, among other places. *Hydra,* a collection of stories that played around with Greek myths. There was *Rubicon Bright.* Not a novel about Julius Caesar crossing the Rubicon. Rubicon Bright was a guy who transgendered. She had wanted to get as far out of her own head as she could. *Something to Behold* was more short stories, this time about people being amazed or fascinated or joyful about something. People always said the short story had to be about loss or death; she'd challenged herself to write a collection in which all the endings would be happy, the characters content. *For the Love of Pete,* a comic novel about a man (Pete) and the woman (Harriet) who loves him. Someone had called her from Los Angeles to say she wanted to take an option on this—for a month, for one hundred dollars. The closest she ever got to fame and fortune. *City Sleeping in the Moonlight Glare.* She had found that title in a poem by Zbigniew Herbert. Her dystopia. The sleeping city was somewhat Kafkaesque.

Two collections published by the university press. Interviews, one-offs, and like that. Then: *Aliens at Home: New and Selected Short Stories.* And: *The Collected Stories of Nina Bryant.* This too was published by the university press, as an e-book. She just couldn't think of it as a real book, even though friends said she should. How can it be real if you can't find it in a real store? she asks them. Her friends remind her that real stores are vanishing. Whereupon she says she needs a drink. Finally, *The Visitors,* a novel. The most recent. It scared her to write this one. She had felt herself broaching an unremittent blackness, a dark with no light in it anywhere, no shading, no relief. Stop spooking yourself, she told herself while she was working on it; you'll be in that place soon, for good. There's nothing scary about it. But still it scared her.

Nina wanted to write another story. She knew it would be her last story, and because of this she was afraid to start it. Tap tap tap went the keys of her computer, but too often she was on the Internet instead of writing. Yet she was determined to write the story. How could she reconcile these two opposing intentions, to write and not to write?

She posed the question to Palmer. "Write it in bits," he suggested. "A paragraph here, another there. All of the important stuff will be in it but you won't think of it as an unfinished whole, because it won't be a whole."

She thought this was a good suggestion and she took it. Paragraphs accumulated in Word.

> The sky's gray light glimmered where clouds parted. The black walnut tree was bare, its hard, fallen crop scattered under snow. A small prancing dog, towed by its owner, peed a bright yellow puddle at the base of the linden tree. Its owner was a woman named Nina. She lived in a brick house on Highland Avenue.

Again:

> Nina taught creative writing and had thousands upon thousands of student stories to read and mark up, or so it seemed to her. Why did so many want to write? Was it in the Zeitgeist? Did they want, as Freud said, fame, fortune, and women? But many of them *were* women. Some of them had trust funds. And a writer's fame was not

> the fame of a rock star. There were no groupies. Maybe one or two, maybe three, but that was it. Could all these young writers be as devoted to writing as she had been, writing not for money or sex or to be admired but writing without acknowledgment, without advances, never knowing whether her current book would find a publisher? *Yes*, she thought, *they could be*, and because of that she read each student's story closely, attending to punctuation as well as structure, to syntax and spelling, to beginnings, middles, and the end. The end of a story should summarize or subvert or cast in a new light everything that had gone before. Though sometimes a story can be like a chapter.

Was it foolish of Nina to use her own name in her story? Norman Mailer had used his. She remembered a phrase from a novel by Phillip Routh (not Roth): "The main purpose of one's double was to show you yourself, or what you're about to become." He'd definitely be more famous if he had changed his name to Philip Roth. Maybe, after all, she would change the name in her story. Diana was a good name. But she'd worry about this later. It didn't really matter what name she used. A rose by any other name.

A third paragraph:

> Her husband is / her husband is / kind / one of a kind / sorrowful / a gentleman / gentle / humorous / as a child she had a miniature silver-plated horse she named Humoresque, after the music / after the music stops / the end of music / of writing / the end of wifehood / the end of mothering / her mother at the end of her life still missed *her* mother / Grandma Hattie / still loved her father / the music-loving sawyer who courted Hattie with grapes / wrath? No / a soft answer turneth away / she is turning away leaving / leaves fresh air the taste of cold air the wind snow / snow draped on windowpanes / heaped beside the road / the road / the road / where is she going?

This third paragraph evokes from her a feeling of further confusion, a sense that syntax has divorced her, left her without alimony. She has to make do with common parts of speech. Cut corners. Trim her sails. She might see syntax again, at a party or the annual AWP conference, but it would be from across the room and they would have only a nodding acquaintance.

Her cell rang. It was Sarah. Sarah vibrated with energy. Nina could feel the little shocks of Sarah's energy bombarding her fingertips as she held the phone. She knew she was fortunate to have such a good and energetic friend.

"What kind of day are you having?" Sarah asked.

"It's okay."

"I saw Cliff this morning."

"Who?"

"Cliff. Maybe you don't remember him."

"Of course I remember him."

"His hair is white. Otherwise, he looks the same."

"Cliff."

"Yes."

"Cliff the geneticist."

"Yes."

"Cliff the cheater."

"That's right."

"Cliff."

"The one and same."

"Don't tell me."

"Okay. I won't."

"Tell me."

"At Bahn Thai." Bahn Thai had the best satay in Madison.

"With?"

"Nobody."

"Did you talk?"

"Yes. He's retired. He's still married to the Canadian."

"*I'm* still married. I don't care if he is."

"He said he broke up with you because he realized his life was going in a different direction."

"Oh god," Nina said. "I'm dying and you're making me feel all these feelings that are completely not in the least at all relevant now."

"I'm sorry. I thought you'd want to know. You were friends."

"Were we? We were lovers. That's different." She said this even though she knew that Sarah had a knack for retaining her former lovers as friends and even though she admired her for it.

Nina reached for the bottle of pain pills on her nightstand. She remembered making love with Cliff in this room. It occurred to her that back then she hadn't even known what love was, so how could she call him "lover"? He was just a guy. And now a white-haired guy.

Age-reversal, that was the hot new development in genetics. Cliff had sponsored his own age-reversal, known as a midlife crisis.

She wasn't the only person dying. Her generation was dying. Friends, the friends of friends, the stars and athletes and politicians of a generation. They would leave nothing behind. A few scraps, perhaps, a film or a treaty or a memo that had wound up in the back of someone's desk drawer. Children were their real legacy, and what they would make of their parents' world was anybody's guess.

"You were lucky to find Palmer," Sarah said, her voice sotto voce and wistful.

"It was a miracle," Nina said, "or at least something like a miracle." She was starting to feel sleepy, the result of the medicine. She told Sarah goodbye and closed her eyes.

As if she were watching a preview, she dreamed of a long tunnel and a white light at the end of it. As she walked, or rather, floated down the tunnel, her feet an inch or two above the floor, she passed scenes from her own life: learning to tie her shoelaces (a belated triumph, that); fitting pegs in holes (an I.Q. test in elementary school); heavy petting in the back seat of a Studebaker with a basketball player; her brother's second wife placing BB's unwanted baby in her arms; Palmer; her parents dying. Was she dying? Was that what was happening to her now? She saw people on the far side, in the light. The closer she got, the sweatier she became. She kicked off the blanket she'd pulled up from the foot of the bed. She had to fight the medicine in her veins. She forced her eyes open.

Nothing was changed. She was alive. There was no one else in the bedroom. The cell phone rested on a pillow. The clouds continued to precipitate but now sleet was falling, small hard bits of sleet peppering the panes, the roof. She couldn't really hear it, but she could see it, and she remembered the curiously comforting sound of rain on a roof or sleet on the windows. She got out of bed. In pajama pants and tee-shirt, she went downstairs to the couch. She didn't believe in tunnels or that Jesus would arrange his schedule to meet her at the end of one. Not unless there were hundreds of thousands of Jesuses, one for every dying person on the planet.

The living room was too dark too early. Traffic on Highland was snarled, tires spinning, horns honking, windshield wipers frantic and falling behind in the effort to keep the windshields clear. She knew this without looking out the front door, because she had lived in Wisconsin for so long that Virginia, once home, seemed a galaxy away. Ithaca and Louisiana—other galaxies. She was a member of Planet Wisconsin now. She would die here. But maybe not on such a cold, lifeless day, maybe on one of those Wisconsin days when the sun is so bright that it bounces off snowbanks and blinds you. She would prefer it to be one of those days.

When did her home become Wisconsin? And had something in her, in her southern-born self, needed the harsh weather, the temperatures so cold that weather reporters informed the citizenry when to bring pets indoors so they wouldn't freeze to death? Maybe she had needed that kind of battle in her life. It was a battle that kept midwesterners alert and ready. Locust plagues, blizzards, tornadoes, deer leaping across highways—midwesterners learned not to take anything for granted. If the sky turned green, they knew to head for the shelter.

When she had, she thought, about fifty or sixty paragraphs, she would figure out how to sort them into a story. And if that didn't work, she could just shuffle paragraphs like cards and call it "A Sort of Story." Or maybe "A Story of Sorts" would be better. There were so many ways of being a writer.

She reached for her notebook. Another paragraph:

> Flannery O'Connor said, "Anybody who has survived his childhood has enough information about life to last him the rest of his days," which was a great line but not entirely true as an assertion. Or rather, the survivor of childhood had enough information but not all the information. Flannery herself could not have known this because she died at thirty-nine, too young to discover that age brings insights unavailable earlier on. Age teaches us something about serenity. Not that one sails through one's last years serenely but that serenity exists within and can sometimes be called upon. Age teaches humility, not the humiliation of youth but the humility of understanding that one is merely one in generations upon generations. Age teaches the artist the freedom of her experience and expertise. And as the senses grow rusty, the pleasure attached to what they register increases. Exhilaration and exultation are even more intense than they were. The old are not bored; they are not bored by anything. Time whips by, leaving boredom in the dust. Age revises the past; it brings new vitality even to forgotten dreams. Yes, for many, possibly most, the alterations age makes will not last until the end. There is no paradise on earth. But we are given a glimpse of paradise before the sky turns dark, and that brief glimpse is sufficient to make sense of everything that came before. How can this information be left out of books? It can't be; it mustn't be. The young need to know these things.

She thought for a bit and then wrote some more:

> And if they roll their eyes when you tell them that, you can always throw in a blowjob.

She thought further:

> That time goes faster as we age is a great boon. It means that when someone close to you dies, you don't spend the rest of your life mourning. Well, in some sense you do, but in another sense, it seems as though just a few days ago you were having a conversation with the dead person. The dead are not dead at all; they are alive and well and having a riotous time in your own mind. And the twenty years that have passed since they died are at most a long weekend. This was Nina's Theory of Thanatology.

She turned on all the lights in the living room, chasing the shadows away. More and more, she felt the need to see things clearly, or as clearly as her cataracts would allow.

Palmer was at the door, fumbling with the lock. She got up and opened the door for him. He was standing there with housekey in one hand and a fir tree—a smallish fir tree—in the other.

She held the door open while he brought the tree inside. She no sooner shut it than Tavy and Callie came bustling in, noses red, and with ice skates strung around their necks. "We went ice skating!" Callie announced joyfully.

"I see," said Nina.

"Have you ever been ice skating, Grandmom?"

"I used to roller skate."

"Like a skateboard," Callie said.

"More like ice skates but with wheels."

"This is our tree?" Tavy asked. "It's smaller than usual."

"But not small," Palmer said.

It was dark green and had a rich, piney smell. "We're going to put the tree upstairs this year so Nina can enjoy the ornaments."

In the old days, the pre-Palmer, pre-Tavy days, Nina decorated a philodendron and let it go at that.

In the large upstairs bedroom the tree stood next to a north-facing window. Palmer put the computer for Callie under the tree a few days before the holiday. No one mentioned Nina's birthday; it would have seemed grotesque to celebrate it when she was dying. She turned sixty-nine in silence. Which, she thought, was not a bad thing to do. Most of the presents under the tree were for Callie, as Nina, Palmer, and Tavy were not feeling festive. But they had tried to feel festive and so had got presents for one another, but mostly for Callie. Nina gave Palmer a poem. Tavy gave Nina a drawing. Nina gave Tavy a poem. Palmer gave Nina a leather-bound copy of her most recent book, and nobody mentioned that it would soon default to Palmer. Tavy gave her father a drawing, and he gave her canvases. In fact, they were trying so hard to be full of Christmas cheer that a certain melancholy hung at the edges of everything. Nina no longer went downstairs and she drifted between sleep and scribbling or reading. Home Help talked with Palmer about hospice care—the house was noisy and crowded (even without ten babies) and Nina had retreated into a personal quiet, saying little, smiling sometimes but not laughing. Palmer was nervous about sleeping next to her: if he rolled over onto her, he might break bones, he might cause her to suffocate. She was so horribly thin. She was frail, perpetually bruised, and too weak to set the laptop on the bed; he had to do it for her, and put it away when she was done.

For that matter, he, too, was exhausted, his nerves frayed and unraveling. He wanted to be alone with his wife but knew his daughter and granddaughter, in the basement apartment, wanted to be with her themselves. He was immeasurably sad, but he was not depressed, because he knew that what he had achieved was what he had wanted—to be a family man, to be tied to his family, to be needed and tugged at and pulled every which way. This was life and he treasured every moment of it. Though once in a while he wanted to go to a sports bar, nurse a couple of beers, and watch the game.

And then once, as he lay beside Nina, she said, "Why don't you go to a bar, drink some beer, watch a game?"

Home Help had been helpful, but now Nina had a physical therapist who came around to exercise her legs, and a nurse who kept tabs on her pain medicines, and Palmer engaged a masseuse twice weekly to help prevent bed sores, though he himself turned her regularly.

And so they got through Christmas and the winter, but they agreed that she would go to hospice when the time came, and it came at the beginning of April. By then Nina had amassed quite a few paragraphs, though she could not say to what end. Her most recent paragraph had been on the subject of clarity:

> Clarity was what Nina always strove for in her work. She abhorred vagueness, the unnecessarily obscure, pretentiousness, the cheap withholding of information, logic too tenuous to reveal itself to the reader. Style is the struggle for clarity, she knew. Hemingway or Henry James—each tried to get onto the page his vision, and as clearly as possible. A writer has a vision, and it precedes language: there are no words for it. She spends her time on earth in search of the right words and the right rhythms for them, that is, the words and rhythms that will convey her vision. To do that is to achieve clarity, and although not everyone in her time will recognize it as

> clarity, someone will, someday. But she had failed to give clarity its due when it came to life. She saw now that without clarity, charity was hit or miss. Without clarity, the true was overshadowed by the meretricious.

At her request, Tavy printed out the paragraphs for her one to a page. Nina had spread them out on the blanket, hoping the right order would manifest itself, when the ambulance—no sirens, no bells or whistles—arrived at the house. It was a rule, at least of the hospice Palmer chose, that patients be transported by ambulance. Or maybe it was an insurance company that required this, since what did they not require?

Palmer collected the paragraphs and put them in a manila envelope to take to hospice. He was thoughtful that way. He knew that even if she couldn't sort them into a story she would want to have them nearby. Inspiration might strike, even in hospice.

"Inspiration might strike. That's my Theory of Literary Theory," Nina whispered to Palmer. She could only whisper now. It took more strength than she had to speak any louder.

April in Madison usually featured a snowfall or two—occasionally a blizzard—but the air was warming. She felt it on her face, that awakening after long sleep. The crocuses and jonquils and tulips that bordered the front of the house were beginning to bloom. The ambulance arrived while Callie was at school. The attendants put her in the back of the van. Tavy kissed Nina on her cheek and Palmer got into the vehicle with her. Tavy ran back into the house, maybe so Nina wouldn't see her crying. Palmer held Nina's hand as the ambulance made its way through traffic.

Palmer's Method of Penmanship

Palmer drained his Scotch in a single gulp. He followed that with another, and then a third. His drinking was deliberate and intentional: he was doing what was necessary to get drunk.

Maybe other husbands wouldn't have to get drunk before they could write a eulogy to their wife. Not he. This was not an operation he could carry out without first anesthetizing himself.

He wrote with a fountain pen. He used real ink. Black.

From his desk he could see, out the window, snow falling on Joss Court. It made him think of James Joyce's story "The Dead." It made him think of Northumbria in the eighth century. He had published a book on Northumbria in the eighth century.

That was the rum thing about being a historian: everything reminded you of something else. His head was overrun with references. He had lived his life in the past tense. He made an effort now to create a portrait of his wife as irreplaceable, beyond substitution, unique, and present. Which, in his mind, she was—as present as she had been for all the years he had known her. He thought back to their first meeting, at the Merchants' Parade with its array of clever floats. He began to write:

When I met Nina for the first time and told her that I could be in love with her, I certainly did not mean that I was. Who falls in love at first sight? Okay, Dante, but who else? I had seen her photograph in her books, of course, but I wasn't in love with a photograph. Maybe with the words? Anyway, what I meant when I said that to her was what I said: that I could be, in time, if things worked out.

As for the notion of "falling in love," it's my impression that for the most part people don't fall in love. What they do is decide to be in love and then talk themselves into being in love with so-and-so. It's a type of self-hypnotism.

That's the way it is for a man, at least. It doesn't mean you wouldn't give your life for the one you've chosen. I'd have given up mine in a second to save Nina's.

The child was a bonus. That was what I wanted: a family, a life outside my work. A forbearing woman who would stick around for the duration.

That day at the Merchants' Parade, when Tavy got lost in the crowd and I grabbed hold of her for Nina, what I saw was a woman with red-brown hair, in one of those summery sorts of dresses—it was sleeveless—and sandals, and she kept turning her head to look for her daughter so I saw her profile. Do you remember Geneviève Bujold? She had Geneviève Bujold's profile. In the Hermitage in Saint Petersburg I saw a painting by Picasso of a woman in medieval dress, including one of those tall cone-shaped hats called a hennin, with a veil trailing from it. Nina looked like her, too.

She was worried sick that Tavy was lost. Or kidnapped. My guess is that the adrenaline rush caused by that is what made her connect with me.

But I would never have told her that. I just said we had chemistry.

I became a historian because I wanted to know what had happened in the world before I arrived. I chose British history rather than American because there's more of it. I chose medieval history because I had seen Picasso's medieval lady and had fallen in love with it. At least I didn't simply do a dissertation in whatever area my director said one could find jobs in. Many dissertators do. *What fascinates you?* I ask my students. *What do you find mysterious and intriguing? That is what you ought to write about. That is where your energies should go.*

I accepted the job here because they gave me a research professorship. Fewer students, more money, more time for my own work.

I cringe inwardly when I use the word "work." Teaching is an easy life for some of us. Not so for those lower on the totem pole. A real person—I use the word "real" decisively, knowing that I am, or was in danger of becoming, one of the unreal—a real person would be justified in asking what we are being paid for. My father was a construction worker, and I know what real people do for a living. What they don't do is read books, present papers, edit volumes of essays on *The Divine Comedy* or *La Vita Nuova*. They don't sit in front of the fireplace, a brandy in hand, imagining what it was like to be a scribe or tutor in the days of the Venerable Bede. They don't have offices with the latest computer equipment, and a rug on the floor, and on the walls rubbings taken at Canterbury. They have money problems. One day they lose their footing on a roof and land in the hospital. While they're lying in bed in the hospital, they have a stroke. They go on disability. They lose their teeth, their sense of self, their temper. Yes, they lose their temper and rise up out of the chair, yelling in a hoarse voice the handful of curse words they can remember after the stroke at their wife and their son, who is still pampering himself in grad school, and keel over with a heart attack and die. That's the life of a real person.

Things had gotten so comfortable for me I was bored. Not with my work, exactly—I could never be bored reading the past—but with the peripherals: the byzantine administration; the tenure deliberations, which were more like turkey shoots than faculty meetings; even, I'm sorry to say, the students. Not with them as people, but they kept asking the same questions, each new class, each new seminar, each new term. I had a reduced teaching load, but at that point I would have preferred none. My first wife must have been just as bored. When she told me she was in love with a woman, my first thought was, How *interesting*.

I guess something had been building up between us for years. I don't know how I could have been so oblivious, except that I had become convinced that my life was how it was and that was all there was to it, nothing would ever change and, all things considered, I had nothing to gripe about.

"A woman?" I asked.

"Yes," she said. "But it's immaterial whether she's a woman or a man. The point is, I'm in love with somebody else."

Dorrie and I met at Stanford. I was an associate professor and she was in law school. We kept waiting for the children to come but it wasn't happening. By the time she made her announcement, it had been not happening for twelve years. She was wearing pajama bottoms and a purple tee-shirt that said GIRLS RULE. Her hair was in a jumble of curls, clipped on top of her head with a clip that looked like a belt buckle. She was tall and slender and pretty and barefoot. I stood there staring at her silver toenails. A lawyer with silver toenails. She started coffee. I felt as if I'd taken one in the gut. I couldn't come up with the breath to talk.

She plucked toast from the toaster. She hadn't really looked at me. She sat down at the kitchen counter on one of the bar-stool-type chairs that came with it and swiveled one way to reach the margarine and the other way to get a knife and then back. Swivel, swivel, like that.

"You're a lesbian?" I finally got out.

"I don't know, Palmer," she said. "Maybe. Maybe I just fell in love and she happens to be a woman. It's hard to know."

"What about me?"

"I know. That's a problem."

"I am not a problem," I said, I thought with some dignity.

"I didn't say *you*. The fact that I'm married to you."

"That's a problem?"

"You don't expect me to stay married to you under these circumstances, do you?" She got off the stool to bring back the coffee pot. She filled cups for both of us.

"It's unclear to me as yet exactly what *these circumstances* are."

When academics have marital spats, they can use up hours defining their terms. Sometimes they can avoid the issue altogether, doing that. Believe me, I know.

She said, "The main circumstance is that I want a divorce so I can live with my lover."

Lawyers, on the other hand, tend to cut to the chase.

I had thought I was fairly self-aware, a conscientious and good if not gifted teacher, a liberal, agnostic (with unacted-upon high-church leanings, which are not uncommon in Medievalists), an advocate of women's rights, kind to dogs and cashiers, a long-suffering fan of the Green Bay Packers, author of several books among which were perhaps a half-dozen significant chapters, not someone who picks a fight and not someone who backs down from one. Marriages have rough patches, but if you hang in there, it's like tracing a sine curve—up and down but holding steady. The best of all possible worlds, I always thought, would be *steady*. And if the price for that was a certain amount of boredom, I would pay it.

So I was surprised by how hurt I was when Dorrie said she was leaving me for a woman. That it was a woman *did* matter; it mattered tremendously. It made me feel that in her eyes I'd never existed. The whole marriage had been *faux*. It was an imitation of marriage, a gesture in the direction of marriage, a sketch of a marriage, but it had not been an actual, undeniable marriage.

Is this homophobic of me? I don't think so. I'm all for gay marriage, I don't see why gay couples shouldn't have the rights and responsibilities of straight couples, if that's what they want. But I wasn't in a gay marriage. I was in what was supposed to be a straight marriage, and my wife wanted to turn her back on twelve years of shared days and nights. It knocked the stuffing out of me. I asked her to think it over, make sure she really wanted to do this. "I already have," she said. "I've been moving toward this decision for a year." She reached for the cordless phone, punched in a number. A one-digit number. She had her girlfriend on speed dial. "Ruth," she said, "I've told him. You can come over now."

Ruth arrived so quickly I wondered if she'd been waiting outside on our stoop. She was wearing a sarong and a ring on every digit. That's what it looked like, anyway. Dorrie told me later that the two thumb rings were actually tattoos.

Why the sarong? I didn't ask.

I shook hands with Ruth, her rings digging into my palm. "Nice grip you have there," I said. Why wouldn't I say that? The woman had brass hands.

"I'm a masseuse," she said.

You'd have to be a masochist to let her give you a massage.

"So," she said. "Are we straight?" Which seemed to me a pretty funny thing to say, considering, but she and Dorrie were somewhere beyond the reach of humor. They had an agenda and were intent on seeing it ratified.

"Not so fast," I said. "You have to understand this comes as a surprise to me."

"Oh, Palmer," my wife said. "How surprised can you be, really?"

"I would have expected a man. So, were you faking it all those years?"

Dorrie glared at me. "Maybe I was."

"Didn't seem so at the time," I said. Mildly, I thought.

"At the time I didn't know myself as well as I do now."

"So I'm surprised, is all," said I.

"I guess it's the male ego, Ruth," Dorrie said, turning away from me and toward her. "I guess you're a challenge to his masculinity."

"Fuck yes," I said. And to tell the truth, I was thinking, What masculinity? I felt about as masculine as a dildo.

Dorrie and Ruth moved to Taos, and I had to fend for myself. And I know my way around a kitchen. I'm no celebrity chef, but I can cook for myself. But the house felt empty, and indeed Dorrie had taken all her stuff and half of what we owned together. I even missed her colorful bottles of nail polish. I hated living alone. I didn't want to live like a monk, and not only for the obvious reason. I wanted to be known as a person, not just a scholar or teacher or tax-paying citizen. I didn't want to be anonymous to myself. It's good, or at least it's good for me, to be around someone who reminds me that I'm in the room with them, with her. It makes me feel real in a way that I don't think my father ever thought I was. Or maybe he did when I was an infant, but from there on he was exhausted after a day of hard labor and while he would have passed a football to me if I had asked, I didn't want to catch a football, I wanted to read. But a wife touches your face, you know you exist.

I didn't want to date a grad student. Grad students live in a state of hushed terror. They are scared their scholarship isn't good enough, they're scared they might discover they don't want to be scholars, they're scared they won't get jobs, they're scared of leaving school and scared of staying in it.

I'd read Nina's books. It seemed to me she knew a thing or two about life. At the same time, I didn't want to know about life. I wanted to live it. She wasn't married, I knew that. There had been some gossip about her, but hey, nobody gossips like academics and there was gossip about every unmarried woman in the department and for that matter every unmarried man. You might think people who refuse to believe anything unless it comes from original sources and is accompanied by footnotes would pay no attention to gossip but it's just the opposite. The more unbelievable the allegation, the more my colleagues believe it. I suppose gossip's a kind of entertainment, like mystery novels and movies. Though there are movies I swear by. Did you ever see *The Horse's Mouth*, the movie based on the Joyce Cary novel? Alec Guinness is brilliant in that, playing an old scoundrel, a con artist who's a real *artist*, and whoever decided to quote from Prokofiev's *Lieutenant Kijé* was equally brilliant.

Palmer reached for his drink only to discover that both bottle and glass were empty and that his mind was wandering. When he came back from the bathroom, he was determined to focus.

I was at the Square that day because I wanted to get out of my empty house. The meeting with Nina? I guess I could say that's history.

After we were married, and I found to my delight that I was the father of a five-year-old girl, we hit a certain rhythm. On weekdays, we kept apart as much as we could, wanting to be independent as teachers. I spent a lot of my day in a different building anyway, at the Institute for Research. This gave me a sweet perspective from which to see her. She'd appear on the Union Terrace, lounging in one of those copyrighted Terrace chairs, and I would think, Hel*lo*, I'm married to that woman! Sometimes she showed up dressed like a professional educator, in a tailored suit, say, or a narrow skirt and a blouse. Sometimes, especially on the days she taught her creative writing workshop, she came to meetings in jeans and one of the ancient sweaters that were her security blankets. I liked seeing her that way, from a kind of distance—as if I were seeing her for the first time. It just created these little moments of surprise, you know? Little electric moments.

While we were at work, our daughter, Tavy, was at school. After some initial resistance to me—I'm sure she thought I might be getting between her and her mother—she began to think of me as her father.

Palmer put down the pen to remember Tavy as a child, her neediness, her willfulness, her quick intelligence. He remembered her visits to his office at school, a little girl who sat on the floor and looked at the pictures in his books of medieval art. He took up his pen again.

This was a hugely meaningful experience for me. Not only did I exist, I felt essential. A man should have children if he can; it makes a grownup of you.

So there we were, the three of us, ensconced in our house on the near West Side, writing and reading books and now and again having one published, and our neighbors were great people and Madison, Wisconsin, ineluctably itself, was never less than amusing, and Tavy was growing up, and that's how it was for us for some years. We had our vacations. We spent a sabbatical year in England. (Nina's parents, who moved there when they retired, had died there, and that year was hard on her. She kept having dreams about them. In her dreams, she was always trying to go to them but she missed the plane or she had forgotten to exchange her money or she couldn't remember their phone number. In her dreams, her parents were lonely and wanted her to come be with them.) We spent a summer in France, and another sabbatical year in Italy. The academy's version of the good life.

Tavy went off to Evergreen College, a fairly experimental school in Washington State, for two years, then came back and enrolled at

UW–Madison. She would have nothing to do with the departments of English and History: too much family for her. She studied art, the history but primarily the practice of it.

That Joyce Cary novel I mentioned—the protagonist was a painter. But I'm happy to say that Tavy is not an old scoundrel. Though she likes to break rules. Tavy has always broken rules. Nina admired that in Tavy, even if it sometimes drove her to distraction. She didn't want her daughter's spirit to be tethered.

She felt hers was. By the university, mostly. She would have liked to have her time for writing. Maybe she could have let me support her, but she was so close to getting her pension, and after years of marking up papers she felt she deserved that.

I'm a scholar, and I know what scholars think of writers. What are writers doing on a campus? is one thing they think. For another, they like to think that writers write by instinct. They don't. I've watched Nina write, and I know that writers practice, practice, practice, just like musicians who hope to get to Carnegie Hall, and revision, Nina's favorite part of writing, is a process of painful self-examination. Finally, scholars often think commentary is more valuable than text, and I suppose one *could* argue that the world already has all the texts it will ever need. Nina was well aware that one could say that. I want to believe that she came to realize what she accomplished, but it's hard to tell. Nor can I pretend to know what her work will mean to the future but when I read her poems I know they change me. They bring me to a place of white light where the world is exposed, where the bones of the world are X-rayed and visible. Our daughter has some of that ability, I think. She has been doing paintings based on some of Nina's poems, which is interesting inasmuch as more commonly poems are based on paintings.

At this point, I was content. My life had turned out better than I had expected it to be and yet it was stable. A wife, a daughter, teaching, research, and writing, everything going smoothly. Then Tavy broke the rules. She got pregnant by a guy she had no wish to marry, and conscious of what Nina had gone through trying to have a kid, she carried the baby to term. (I really must be medieval, because my first reaction was to want to sock the guy who knocked her up.) We now had a painter and a baby in the family. Painters need money for materials and at the start of their careers are likely to have none. We told her she could live with us until she could make it on her own. We gave her the basement to live and paint in. That's worked out well. I put up a partition between the studio and her very small bedroom and made sure the studio was adequately ventilated; none of us wanted to expose the baby to even the vaguest drift of paint. Nina and I loved having our granddaughter under our roof. Tavy named her Callie.

Callie has her grandmother's/great-aunt's brown eyes, dark brown hair and a high brow. In fact, she looks very much like Nina in Nina's childhood photos except that her skin is darker. She's smart and gives the impression that something is always on her mind but rarely says what. She loves the violin. She definitely carries the gene for music, no doubt from Nina's parents. I was assigned to the bassoon in junior high but, again, preferred reading. Plus, we weren't allowed to take the instruments home so I never got very far with it. This was no loss to the music world.

Callie has her own quarter-size violin and plays it every day. She'll need a half-size soon, but not yet. She's small. When she's finished, she carefully wraps it in a satin scarf Nina got for her for this purpose before setting the violin in its case. The scarf is a creamy white and is beautiful against the polished wood of the fiddle. Callie calls the fiddle her *most cherished possession* but before long she's going to want something that sounds better.

Callie also insists that we call her babysitter her *companion.*

We take Callie with us when the Pro Arte plays, and she sits on the edge of her chair and watches and listens as if nothing else exists, not even us. It's the same way at the Choral Union concerts. It's odd how families repeat themselves, isn't it? Thus, Tavy clearly inherited her talent for visual art from Nina's brother.

In my own family, we never had a clue as to who might have had this or that talent. We were just people struggling to get by. No music lessons, no canvases or paintbrushes to express yourself with; no chemistry sets, for that matter. I got books from the public and school libraries, and I had a free ride through college thanks to a Regents Scholarship, which was thanks to my having been born in upstate New York. Very different from Dorrie's family, which was all about lawyering and doctoring. Her folks gave her everything she wanted, and when she hooked up with Ruth, they gave her new china as a starting-over gift. A starting-over gift! Hallmark should start a line of cards.

I trust I don't sound envious or angry, because I'm not. God knows, I don't need new china. I don't need old china, either. Paper plates. On the whole I am a paper plate kind of guy. I don't mean that literally, but I'm pretty easy-going. For just that reason, some people might have found it strange that Nina and I got on so well together, but underneath the anxiety she had a streak of easy-goingness herself. I sensed that in her.

People thought she was—how to say this?—that she was *hounded* by her ambition, as if the dogs of war, or in this case writing, were nipping at her heels. But this is simply not true. She was simply dedicated. She had ideas for books and felt she owed it to the ideas to realize them. What made it look like she was constantly goading herself on was that she had so *many* ideas. Now, you either have a lot of ideas or you don't, and if you do, you're stuck with them. She felt obligated to accommodate them, since, of course, nobody else would, short of a roomful of monkeys typing ad infinitum.

One time she woke me up in the middle of the night to tell me she was worried about getting all her books written. "What can I do?" she asked.

"Prioritize," I said.

I remember it was autumn but still warm and the window was open. There were already a couple of cars parked in front of our house, football fans making sure they had parking places for the game that afternoon. Our house is near the stadium.

Palmer put the pen down, wondering if he should write our house is *or* our house was *or* my house is. *He was feeling the effects of the whisky. But, he told himself, the first bottle had not been full, and he would allow himself just a few sips of the new one, which he had pulled out of his filing cabinet.*

I had gotten out of bed and gone to the window and noticed all this when I heard her say, "That's like deciding who gets to live and who dies, Palmer. Like a Roman emperor. How can I make that kind of decision?"

"You'll make it anyway," I told her. "If you prioritize, at least you'll be thinking the choices through and not just flying by the seat of your pants."

Love is hard. Two people trying to walk side by side on a busy sidewalk, that's what love is. People get in the way. There's that little dance people do when someone comes directly toward them and neither knows what side to veer to. Or someone races ahead and blocks the view. Or the light changes to red before you get across the street.

Then again, I would get into my work, and Nina would go into hers so deeply that sometimes I thought of her as Persephone. I had her part of the year, and the rest of the time she was in the depths of her mind. She loved to write. She may have felt an urgency about her books, but she absolutely loved the act of writing, especially when she could lose herself in it. "Writing is like living in eternity," she said.

"Time takes place *in* what you are writing but there is no time *while* you are writing, because you are not there to experience it. Only the writing exists." She never rushed it.

Nina didn't live *only* in her writing. She had a full life. She gave the credit for this not to me or even Tavy but to the little dog she had when I met her. It was a male cairn terrier, salt and pepper, furry, with red whiskers and—she said—the cutest butt she'd ever seen. I had to agree: he had a saucy prance when he trotted. She always said it was her dog who taught her how to trust and care for someone else, that she would not have been able to raise Tavy or marry me if it hadn't been for that little dog. She said it was the dog that had helped her to negotiate her way from desperation to serenity. The Nina I know did have a serene air about her, even with the anxiety and the crushing need to find time to write. I don't mean she achieved nirvana or smiled like a Bodhisattva. And she didn't have it *all* the time. Serenity, like a marriage and the moon, waxes and wanes. But she had it. It was as if she had let go of a lot of peripheral stuff and understood she was doing what she was meant to be doing: writing.

Like Tavy, the dog, small as he was, was stubborn, and like her, he resented me for a while at first, but he was too happy a dog to sulk for long. He and Tavy slept on the same bed, and Nina and I would find them in the morning with both their heads on the same pillow.

Palmer paused, calling the picture of the twosome to mind. One of them had been at the beginning of her life and the other was approaching the end of his. He remembered that he had gotten an actual ache in his heart looking at them. Fatherhood, he thought, had been the miracle in his life. As for the dog, a dog was a dog, but he respected the feelings his wife and daughter had for their dog, and he was willing to admit that there were times when the cute canine sat beside him in the Green Bay Packers chair while he was reading—usually history or something Nina wanted his response to—and he'd had the haunting sense that the creature already knew what was in the book. It was true that he had seemed quite knowledgeable for a dog, as if he'd gone places and seen things that most people haven't. Or maybe it was just that it was a relief to have another male in the house.

Nina liked dogs in general, but she was partial to those small enough to hold in her arms. There is no question that she thought of her dogs as her children. "How can other people have the slightest idea of what I feel for my dog?" she'd ask. "And how many people treat their children like dogs, and I don't mean the way I treat dogs?" Nina used to say that if there was a heaven and dogs were not permitted, it could not be heaven. She'd say that *dog* is a synonym for *soul*. I understand what she meant. Saint Paul never had to preach to dogs. Dogs come into the world already knowing what Paul was talking about, though that knowledge can be beaten out of them.

If anybody wants to make a charitable contribution to dogs on Nina's behalf, I know she would appreciate that.

After Tavy arrived, though, Nina told me, man's best friend became more her dog than Nina's. He was slowing down, though his prance endured until his final week. I remember how Nina would burst out laughing with pleasure just watching him prance. It lifted her heart. She thought he was beautiful. He was certainly cute. Nina had a great laugh, she always gave herself to it whole-heartedly. When she laughed, I laughed, and I'm not sure I ever had before, not a full-bore all-out laugh. Until Nina, I was a chuckler, which is to say, a bemused critic. That is, I was above the fray, above the laughter. Nina brought me into the fray. And the laughter.

The death of the dog was for Nina the end of an era. But other dogs followed, and a few years ago, we brought home a bichon puppy, a trembly ball of white fluff—he seemed to be wearing a coat made of cotton balls—and we named him Wolf, because, as Nina said, he was in sheep's clothing. Wolf is as adulatory and obedient and eager to please as the cairn terrier was strong-willed and self-directed, and when Tavy was making art or looking after Callie, he'd lie on Nina's lap as she worked at her desk.

One day when I was out Wolf skidded down the stairs, sliding down some of them, barking his head off. Tavy followed him upstairs to Nina's study. Nina was standing next to her printer, leaning over and holding her stomach. Tavy saw the depth of pain and a hint of panic in Nina's eyes and called our doctor. When I got home, I found Nina in bed and Tavy, Callie, and Wolf all on the bed. Oh yes, Callie's teddy bear, a relic from Nina's childhood that had been Tavy's too, was also on the bed. It was a charming scene, not a scary one. A stomach ache. Who *doesn't* get stomach aches? We didn't recognize it as the beginning of the end. Neither did the doctor.

The doctor prescribed ibuprofen and an antidepressant. He told her to take walks, the longer the better, but getting Nina outdoors during the winter was damn near impossible. She'd take the dog out if no one else was around to do it, but she hated the cold, and she considered anything below seventy degrees cold. She was from Virginia and liked to say that the older she got, the colder she got.

Nina knew she was out of shape. She'd tried once or twice to get in the habit of working out at a gym but complained that it took too much time out of her day. And after all, she was nothing like an invalid, and everybody slows down as they age; everybody gets stomach aches from time to time. She kept on meeting her classes and we went to movies and concerts and when Tavy had her first show Nina helped her get ready for it. Nina designed the invitations on her computer.

That was a great evening, that opening. We were both so proud of Tavy we thought our hearts would stop. Simultaneously. We were also surprised—Tavy hadn't shown us the series of drawings she had done using soft graphite on white paper. They were rather threatening works. Blocks of black against the white or vice versa, deserted streets, buildings that might be prisons or secret laboratories, all angles and perspective, without figures. They say something about the deadness of contemporary civilization, maybe that modern technology has made humans redundant. As in the British sense of the word "redundant," where it means not only "unnecessary" but also "let go," "fired," "cut off." Nina buttonholed everyone who came in, giving them a glass of wine and a lecture like a docent. The exhibit was held at the gallery owned by Sarah, Nina's friend who has been so true to her and an aunt to Tavy and was a godmother to our terrier. It was quite a launch party, and Tavy sold a painting and one of the drawings. Nina and I stayed to help Sarah clean up, and when we got home we were happy and tired. I fixed Nina a late drink. She got into bed to read—she was reading *Under the Glacier* by Halldór Laxness—and kept breaking into laughter. Marina Tsvetaeva called laughter "that cheap tambourine"—Nina had read me the poem, the Feinstein translation—but to me it was sublime music. Then she seemed to swallow wrong, maybe because of laughing or maybe because of the Scotch, and started coughing. I've never seen someone have that kind of coughing fit. It sounded like someone was ripping her throat out. The next day the doctor saw us in his office. I was assuming she had chronic bronchitis, or even walking pneumonia.

In fact, the coughing fit was probably unrelated to anything. When someone close to you gets sick, you look back to see when it might have started. But she also told the doctor about her stomach aches. I thought there had been only one, but it turned out she'd been having them all along. She added that she thought she was experiencing something like a malaise. But who doesn't? Isn't that the hallmark experience of our time, knowing no one person can effectuate anything? The doctor urged her to put on a little weight. I was taken aback to see how much thinner she was, but she wasn't . . . wasn't what? She wasn't emaciated. To me, she just looked trim.

"I'm happy I've lost a couple of pounds," she said. "It's too easy to gain it, especially for a writer who sits at her desk all day."

He told her to let him know if she lost any more weight.

It's hard not to blame oneself. You live with someone, you don't notice how they're changing. We were busy. At some point I realized she had lost more weight and I reminded her of what the doctor had said. More time went by. Too much time. This time I was adamant. "You have to call him," I told her. She called him and he told her to come back in.

She climbed on the examination table. This time he felt a mass in her stomach. He ordered tests.

"Not a word to Tavy," Nina cautioned me.

Nina was worrying about stomach cancer. She thought maybe smoking was to blame. She had quit smoking at the age of thirty-two, but for much of her life before and after she was surrounded by smokers. She recalled that the apartments and houses she grew up in were so veiled in smoke you could get lost going from the living room to the dining room. The air in the rooms looked like smog, she said. Nina talked about how her mother had smoked right up till she died. Nina had taken Tavy to England to meet her mother after her father died. Her mother couldn't walk at all anymore and subsisted on hot chocolate, soft-boiled eggs, and cigarettes. Nina pleaded with her mother not to smoke when Tavy was in the room, but her mother said, "If you can't stand the heat, get out of the kitchen," which made no sense because she wanted Nina to make the hot chocolate and even told her she should quit her job and move to England to look after her. I never met Eleanor Bryant but I think I know a lot about her. I've met my share of manipulative narcissists. But Nina loved her mother. She said her mother was afraid, not knowing when death would come for her. Not knowing how it would feel, if it would be painful. There were times when Eleanor could hardly breathe, and Nina saw her mother struggling against suffocation.

I used to think fathers and sons were complicated. Now I think mothers and daughters are even more complicated. How can a daughter break away from the person who has been most with her since the beginning, who is her own image? It's like turning your back on yourself, and where does that take you? It was important to Nina that *her* daughter be free to live her own life. But Nina did not accuse her mother of keeping her from living her life. She accused herself of leaning on her parents for a place to stay and write, since without that help she couldn't have done what she wanted to do. She said she was sure her first four books would not have been written without her parents' support, their willingness to let her live with them. I imagine that's part of why she didn't hesitate when Tavy wanted to stay on at home.

Smoking may or may not have been a factor; there was no way to be sure. The CT scan came back. Then the MRI. Then the ultrasound. The radiologist did a fine-needle aspiration. The tissue was biopsied. What Nina had was pancreatic cancer, and it had already progressed.

I have learned that it is difficult to determine what stage of pancreatic cancer the patient is in. The imaging tests suggested that Nina was in Stage III: the cancer was in her blood vessels but probably not yet in her organs. It was only "locally advanced." This sounded like good news until the doctor told us it meant that she was not "resectable."

I asked him what the hell "resectable" meant.

It meant there was no point in surgery.

He said it was just as well that we knew that now. In half the resectable patients, the surgeon goes in to discover it's already too late. They just sew the patients back up.

He said that for Nina he would suggest *chemotherapy followed by radiation*. "Blast the little bastards out of there," he said. We saw another doctor. He suggested *chemotherapy followed by radiation*. We went back to our first doctor.

He used gemcitabine with the chemo. But the chemo caused nausea and vomiting and fatigue, and she was still losing weight. She also had severe anemia and immune system suppression, which meant she was susceptible to infections. But nothing stopped the progression, including the radiation.

They gave her counseling and more antidepressants, but we knew she was going to die. Was, in fact, dying. It was time to tell Tavy. She knew of course that Nina had lost weight and was sometimes in pain. When I told her what Nina had, she accepted the news quietly. A little sobbing, that was all. Or so I thought. Later I looked for her in the basement and found her not so much painting a canvas as murdering it. It's like a boxing match: the attempt to wrestle pain into art. Yes, I've learned that from my girls.

That day it was snowing and the furnace had gone off and Nina was wrapped in blankets but still cold and trying to write. Nina was so exhausted by this that she was on the verge of tears. The snow sputtered out and the day was so dim and grim, we all wanted to be somewhere else, each of us in a room alone, safe and asleep, and I imagine Nina felt that most of all. I wanted to be somewhere else because I felt so useless. I wanted to make Nina well, and there was nothing I could do.

We sat with her. Callie played the violin for her. I read to her. But despite all the evidence I still had trouble believing that she was dying. How could she be dying? She was right there beside me, asking if I thought she should change the semicolon in line five of the poem about the Shmoo to a period.

Do you remember Shmoon? From Al Capp's *Li'l Abner* strip. Li'l Abner led them out of the Valley of the Shmoon. The strip started a craze for everything Shmoo. In the forties. Nina had a Shmoo toy when she was a child. It was about as tall as she was, a round balloon body with very big eyes painted on the face and with big, flat shoes but no legs. You could knock it back and forth and it would wobble but it wouldn't fall over. Her poem was about that particular Shmoo.

I remember Shmoon well. I read that comic strip when I was a kid. Shmoon lived on air, loved food and loved *being* food. They would do anything for anyone. In 1948 we filled Shmoon with candy and airlifted them to Berlin, where they were dropped behind the Soviet blockade. Their worst enemies were the green Nogoodniks.

But what I mean to say is that, sick as Nina was, she was alive. It's so easy to look at an old person, for example, and assume that they're not fully alive, but you are alive until you are not alive. Nina dying was not less alive or less real. She was my wife, my friend, my daughter's mother, my grand-daughter's grandmom, my colleagues' colleague. I didn't want to think of life without her. I couldn't bear to think of life without her.

She was jaundiced, her very fair skin tinted oddly golden. The pain grew steadily worse.

She needed hospice care. She needed pain relief, a button to push for morphine.

Not at home. She wouldn't have hospice at home. "I don't want Callie to watch me die," she said. "I want her to remember me alive."

We put her work in whatever order we could, and she grieved for the work she had not written.

"You and Tavy will come visit me. Callie, no. No, Palmer."

She said my name like that. *No, Palmer.* I knew I could not refuse her.

We moved her to hospice. Her breathing had changed, the nurse said, and it would be soon—maybe a week, at most two weeks. Tavy and I went to see her. Some of her friends. Sarah, of course. The Wallaces. The Durkheims. *No, he shouldn't say "the Durkheims," because Jazz had kept her own last name.* Quinn and Conrad. Rich and Ingrid. Mary and Sam. Even Hugo Gutsmer, the weird freelance ethicist, who no doubt has spent plenty of time thinking about life and death and the right to life and the right to death but I'll eat my baseball cap if he ever figures anything out. I hung around the whole time he was in the room because god only knew what he'd say to Nina. He didn't, though. He just said goodbye.

I watched him leave, the glass door closing behind him with the rectory hush with which modern door dampers replace loud slams.

"I wanted more time," Nina said, fiercely. "I need more time."

I wanted to give her more time. I wanted to give her eternity.

The nurse was attentive and kind but that didn't prevent Nina's getting pneumonia. She no longer wanted to see her friends, because she couldn't carry on a conversation with them and she didn't want them to have to sit around and just look at her. "That's no way to treat a friend," she said to me, although it was difficult to catch her words. Tavy was there, of course. Tavy showed her mother her newest painting, which was of Nina, from a photograph taken in her thirties. Even without the medieval headgear, the woman in the painting reminded me of the woman in the painting by Picasso.

Nina once told me that when she was a little girl her mother had dressed her in medieval gown and conical hat with silk scarf for a Halloween costume contest. She didn't win, but her mother told her the judges were looking away from the parade when she walked by them.

I didn't have a painting. I could yak about the Northumbrian monastery of Saint Peter at Monkwearmouth or the Arab Empire or the Plague of Justinian, which reduced the population of Europe by half, but no, actually I couldn't. I just held her hand. She died a week later, at about seven in the evening. I am not going to repeat her last words; they were for me only.

Palmer looked up from his writing. He was startled to see that his handwriting had grown wildly large and described a rollercoaster ride, moving sometimes upward and more often downward. He looked at his watch; it was six a.m.

He rose from his desk and went downstairs to feed the lamblike Wolf, then climbed the stairs again and lay down on the bed in the bedroom. He tried not to think about sleeping beside his wife. He woke up at noon, took a shower, shaved, put on a fresh shirt; it felt good to get cleaned up. He went downstairs to make coffee—Guatemalan and black. He returned to his study, cup in hand, sat down at his desk, and read what he had written. Then he tore it up and wrote a serviceable eulogy. By five p.m. his head felt as though someone had buried a hatchet in it.

Epilogue: All the Little Dogs

The little dogs and all,
Tray, Blanch, and Sweetheart, see, they bark at me.

King Lear 3.6

She was sorry not to be able to devote her attention to them but her family would have to understand that she was busy. Her brain had become a staging area for sentences that sped off one after the other, breaking the sound barrier. Only later, after a sentence had left, did she hear the verb's insistent hum or recognize the metallic glint of an adjective. She wanted to say Stop! Stay! I need to parse the syntax, I need to hear cadences a second time. But when she managed to whisper the word "stay," her husband and daughter, or sometimes her friends, pulled their chairs even closer, and of course she loved them but things were different now, they were already learning to live without her, and she—she had a head full of orthographic aircraft, a control tower out of control.

The room was crammed with flowers. The scent of them was on the sheets, in her hair.

She is thinking. That was a sentence, a true one. *She is feeling.* That was also a sentence, not false, but not so true as the first. She felt a kind of pressure, from the air, from her family's presence, from the door that opened and closed, but not much else. *She is sleeping.*

True! she thought, startled to find herself waking—from what dreams? Had she had a dream, or was she asleep for only a second? There was no way of knowing. There were never mealtimes anymore. Breakfast, lunch, dinner—appointments on someone else's schedule, not hers. For her, time was nothing, though it was a continuous nothing, an empty space. Time had ceased to speak to her; it had said all it was ever going to say.

Mute time. That interested her: time without sentences. Without verbs.

Her husband was calling her name. She heard him as from a distance. Just her name, no sentence.

There were all those famous first sentences: *Happy families are all alike; it is a truth universally acknowledged, that a single man in possession of a good fortune, must be in want of a wife; it was the best of times, it was the worst of times; Mother died today*, et cetera, but they belonged to the past. She was in search of sentences that transcended time. Such sentences would have to be made up of nouns. *Husband.* That would be a sentence, and why not, didn't the noun say it all? Her belated, beloved Palmer, arriving on the scene just in time to make her later years joyous, a completely unexpected surprise. *Daughter*—though how could that one word convey her daughter's history as her niece's daughter, or even begin to hint at the whirling entity that was Tavy.

Language would have to give a little, relax the rules, bend to accommodate the new, the complex. Well, that was what languages did, anyway.

She heard thunder followed by lightning: so it was raining. How strange, in her situation, to think of weather. The seasons in Wisconsin: winter and road repair. But fall was often lovely, brilliant leaves, brisk air, the students enthusiastic (for a week or two). Then the football games, with fans parking on Joss Court and all around her house. The long winter a slog, a thing that had to be got through each year, although she knew plenty of people who reveled in it, who went cross-country skiing or ice-fishing or showshoeing and liked the prickly feel of the cold biting their noses, the heat of blood rushing to their cheeks. She wasn't one of them. She missed the South, what it was like to tread barefoot on warm asphalt. Had never gotten accustomed to the cold. In Madison the summers were hot but rather dry. The natives complained about high humidity, but they had no idea what high humidity was. They'd never attempted to roll a piece of paper into a typewriter only to find the paper had turned into a damp rag.

Had Tavy ever seen a typewriter?

Spring in Madison was pretty much a wash. It seemed to happen on a day in mid-May every year, and then it was summer.

And today—a storm. A Wisconsin storm, where the black clouds battled it out with one another, the wind manic with despair, and lightning that slashed the sky the way Tony Perkins had slashed Janet Leigh in *Psycho*.

Her husband stroked her forehead, pushing her hair back from her face.

Weather was always interesting when you were in it. But it was not as interesting as sentences.

Banked in her mind were words she'd wanted to use but never found the sentences for. *Oilily*. He winked at her and asked *oilily* if she'd go out with him. *Idyllically*. *Sontagish*. The middle-aged professor sported a Sontagish streak in her hair. *Wackadoodle*. The guy was wackadoodle. Or should that be *a* wackadoodle?

If you subtracted all the predicates, what would you have if not something like Plato's realm of forms? Unmonitored nouns fixed in place in a place that was no place. And that wasn't very interesting, so she returned to a part of speech that had struck her as rich with possibility: the gerund. People were born verbs, but as they actualized their potential they became more and more gerundive, until, perhaps, they became what they loved to do. Now, she could see right off that there were problems with this. Quite a lot of people would choose simply to have/be sexual congress for eternity. There would be some who'd choose to be evil and a few more whose quirky or weird passions would take them over. But maybe those simply wouldn't enter on eternity, although a harmless quirk—there would have to be operants who could say who was within the guidelines, who not. No, this was getting too complicated.

Maybe the act of killing, for example, grammatically speaking, did not require an actual killed object. People became the doing, not the done to. So now everyone could get in. Murderers, terrorists. Maybe even Republicans. Come one, come all, to Paradise. Theologians would not like that idea. But at least it would mean that God, if there turned out to be a god, was taking responsibility for the mess he'd made!

Would they know where they were? They might be too happy to care; after all, they would all be doing what they most loved to do. She would have an eternity in which to write her sentences. If the thought of that made her just a little bit tired, she would still be living *idyllically.*

Living was the wrong word here; she didn't know what the right word would be.

Tavy sniffled. Nina heard her daughter pull out a tissue and blow her nose. Silly girl. There was nothing to cry about.

When Sarah and Shelley had come to visit, they had sat on the edge of the bed, one on each side, and told her they were glad to have known her. Nina wanted to ask Sarah about the art gallery and Shelley where she and Ian would travel next. Shelley and Ian had so far gone to Machu Picchu, Cornwall, Nairobi, Istanbul, Alaska, and the Seychelles. Their idea was to visit as many places as they could before age caught up with them. Unfortunately, all Nina had been able to say was "Where?" but Shelley understood and said, "Yemen," and Sarah told Shelley she really should put Kashmir and Beijing on her list, and a discussion about visas ensued, which meant Nina didn't have to try to talk.

Nina had not imagined she would be one of those to leave earlier rather than later. She'd been caught by surprise. She had joked that she was counting on a great late age to finish what she'd started. But she'd bet that there had been a good many other writers with the same thought who'd found themselves out of luck. Did it matter? Hell, yes, it mattered. In the history of culture, uncountable numbers of ideas had died unrealized, and every such loss furthered the depletion of the universe, the small absences adding up to a longing felt in every point in space. Was she being overly dramatic? Surely a woman had a right to be a bit dramatic on her deathbed; she'd not been one to dramatize her life. Besides, she believed ideas were valuable and essential. Bad ideas could and did wreak havoc, destroying worlds and species, but that only demonstrated the absolute necessity for countervailing good ideas.

Not that one could know in advance if an idea was good or bad. Not that one could even know afterwards, if one's ideas were realized as art.

We're flying blind here.

Amazing how suggestive language could be: she caught herself thinking she was in the sky, not so much flying as bobbing on blueness, floating on her back on the sea of the sky.

As soon as she thought this, she became once more aware of herself in the bed. A nurse fixed the pillow under her head. Were Palmer and Tavy still there? Hard to tell—the room had become so quiet. She wished someone would play music, a quartet, a Beethoven quartet, that was what she wanted to hear, but it was probably against hospital rules. People ought to be asked what soundtrack they wanted to die to. She was surprised they weren't. Didn't everybody know that the sense of hearing was the last to go? Even for a patient who'd got a little hard of hearing?

There. She could hear the opening bars of the *Grosse Fuge* in her head. That sublimity, that beauty beyond the merely beautiful.

She heard Tavy come into the room. She knew her daughter's light, racing steps, the gazelle, the spinning top that was Tavy. Tavy had brought back food from the cafeteria; she could hear Palmer and Tavy unwrapping sandwiches, Palmer blowing on hot coffee, ice chinking dully against the sides of Tavy's plastic cup. Palmer filled a paper sack with the trash and crushed it in his hand. She tried to smell what they were eating but couldn't. Food itself seemed like an abstraction to her now. She remembered how reluctant her mother had been to eat when she was old and sick. Death: The Easy Way to Diet. She was sad to think she wouldn't see her parents again; that had been such a comforting story, the story of heaven, of resurrection. A whole lot of people had died happily, confident that they would meet their loved ones in another, better place. She didn't expect to run into anyone she knew.

She would have liked to see her parents again, hear them practicing the eleventh, sit with them around the kitchen table, chewing the bones of old philosophical or aesthetic or political dilemmas, the big questions, Watergate on the TV in the house in Richmond, those days when she was a young woman working on her first novel. She would even like to see her problematic brother again, though he had never forgiven her for not allowing him to come live with her after Maureen kicked him out.

But she had no illusions—or as someone else might say, faith. Dust to dust. And in that, too, there was a kind of consolation: an end to suffering, freedom from hope and hopelessness alike, rest. Life was work, hard, hard work. To nap for eternity might not be a bad thing.

Not dead yet, she hoped Palmer would find a wife after her. He was not good alone. He needed someone to talk with, do things with, a woman to anchor him. He had a tendency to drift, forget where he was headed, even where he was. He needed someone to tell him when to buy new shirts, someone to keep him informed about the headlines. He also needed someone to hold in his arms at night. It was the only way he could really be sure that he existed.

But her daughter. What would happen to her daughter, for whom she'd wished so much and had been so deeply grateful. Tavy was not quite the angel Nina had expected she would raise (of *course* all of the love she would bestow on a child would make the child an angel!). Stubborn, determined, emotional, and now a single mother herself. Would she pursue her painting beyond these apprenticeship years? How far could she go? Would she marry? Nina would never know, but then, it was Tavy's life, not hers, and maybe it was better for Tavy that Nina would not be around to have opinions about it.

She remembered her daughter as a small girl sleeping with her teddy bear, that hand-me-down from Nina's own childhood, and Virgil, the little dog who was also a kind of hand-me-down from Nina.

The little dog who had kept Nina company through the roughest years.

Oh, sweet, sweetest Virgil! How she had loved him, how he had rescued her from bitterness and despair! And here he was, again, on the bed, sniffing her hand. She felt the sticky scrape of his small tongue, saw dewdrops of sweat on his funny black nose.

—You came, she said, smiling, and he answered, Have I not always guided you?

—I've been wondering, Virgil.

—What?

—Dante Alighieri called life a comedy, but it's one tragedy after another. How can comedy and tragedy be reconciled?

—Eternity, he said. It takes an eternity to reconcile them. A life of pain, a life cut short, a stunted life—these are mere pratfalls in eternity.

—Where are we going?

—Into your work.

—What does that mean?

—You know exactly what it means. Your father told you when his ghost appeared in the kitchen in England. You are becoming what you have made of yourself.

She warmed her hands in Virgil's thick double coat as if he were a muff.

—Where have you *been*?

—Around. A dog without his mistress just hangs around. And sleeps a lot. But now we need to get a move on.

Virgil's dark-bright eyes gazed at her as when he had lived with her.

—Do you know Blaze and Oscar? she asked, thinking of her parents' dogs.

—Of course. Dogs of a feather flock together.

—You always were a funny guy. And cheerful, very, very cheerful! She hugged him, resting her chin atop his head, and remembered how sad he'd been whenever she had to leave him behind the baby gate when she went to work.

—Hurry up! he said. As if he were tugging at his leash, like the day he broke away and explored most of Madison. Thank god, he'd been waiting for her the next morning, happily surveying the SPCA from the high counter separating staff from the public.

She meant to race out with him right this moment, but the nurse did something to her IV and someone turned the television on, laughter reaching her from a corner of the ceiling, and she could tell time had passed, because it was prime time.

It *was* prime time, and she was wasting it by sleeping. The expense of spirit in a shame of waste. She wanted to stay awake, to be alert to what was happening to her. After all, you only die once—and she laughed to herself.

—I'll wait till you're ready, Virgil said.

While she was asleep, Blaze and Oscar had joined him. All the little dogs in her life.

—Hi, Blaze, hi, Oscar, she said.

—Do you want to see the old man? Blaze, her father's dog, asked.

—Yes, of course, yes, yes. Where is he?

—I'm here, her father said. He was standing behind Blaze, the leash—*lead*, he'd learned to say in England—in his hand. He tugged Blaze back a bit. Blaze's white forehead seemed to shine in the room lit only by the flickering TV. She couldn't see her father very clearly, but she recognized his voice, and in his non-leash-holding hand, he gripped a violin by the neck.

—Oh, play me something! she said. Play the Bach Chaconne.

He did, and the music poured into her mind, a Niagara of notes.

—Where is Mom? she asked, when he had reached the end.

Oscar, the inscrutable Oscar, with his punched-in muzzle and tail like a golden dragon, said that her mother was writing a book called *Do You Want to Live in Heaven?*

—She didn't even believe in heaven, Nina said.

—Maybe not, but she always believed in staying busy. Oscar blinked his Chinese eyes. Her father nodded. Blaze scratched himself.

—Am I just imagining all of you?

—Why do you say "just imagining," Nina? her father asked. I always thought you took imagination seriously.

Virgil nipped at her ankles as if to say, If you could call me up with your imagination, wouldn't you have done so long before now?

—Oh, Virgil, I would have.

—I'm glad you're finally using my name.

—It's such a heavy name for a little dog. I don't know why I burdened you with it. I regretted it right after I filled out your AKC papers.

—I know why you named me that, he said, but her mother came on the scene just then. They watched her type on the ancient manual Remington on which she had once typed dissertations for Cornell students, clicking away on the keys like there was no tomorrow. And, of course, there wasn't.

—There you are, she said. Nina. We've been waiting.

—Am I going to have to deal with all your neuroses forever? Nina asked her, hoping to know from the beginning what the score was.

—Your father doesn't mind.

—Dad has always been patient.

—You put us through the wringer too, if you remember. Besides, everyone learns to be patient here. It's the nature of eternity.

—I thought you'd be playing the violin.

—I do, most of the time. But this book is a natural. Someone had to write it. Did I ever tell you I came in second in the state competition for the fastest typing in Mississippi? I would have won if my father hadn't been standing beside me the whole time, commenting on my every move.

—Where's—

—Your brother? That's still a sore spot.

Virgil barked. His sturdy little salt-and-pepper body, his jaunty tail gladdened Nina's heart.

—What is it? Nina asked.

—We have to keep going, Virgil said.

—But . . . I thought. . . . She had thought they had already arrived somewhere, but as she looked around, everyone began to disappear, her father first, then her mother. Blaze and Oscar ran after them and faded from sight too.

—Come, Virgil said.

The TV had been turned off. Palmer was still there, holding her hand. She wished he would talk to her, but she knew he'd feel odd talking to somebody who didn't respond. She knew also that if she pointed that out to him he would say, What do you think I do in the classroom? Talk to students who show no response!

She missed sleeping beside him. His bulk, the heat of his body, even his snoring if it wasn't too loud made her feel safe, made her feel as if she were guarded by a fortress, as if in the central hearth of the fortress there burned a fire that warmed but would not destroy.

She and Virgil were passing through scenes of incredible beauty. Sometimes people were in them and sometimes she saw only clouds and mountains, or wild grasses and sea oats, or sun on rooftops. At every stop, she felt her heart would burst from a surfeit of beauty.

—But if *everything* is so beautiful, she asked Virgil, how does anyone come to appreciate any of it?

—You don't have to listen to bad music to appreciate Beethoven, he said. You just have to listen to Beethoven.

Now there were stars, stars, and more stars—everywhere. The light from them was cool and blue and distant. She felt she was swimming in stars.

—You're allowed in heaven, Virgil?

—Didn't your father tell you dogs are more than welcome in Paradise?

—He had Alzheimer's. He didn't always know what he was saying.

—Can you really believe that any community based on love would exclude dogs?

Palmer had been holding her hand for so long that she could no longer distinguish between her hand and his. She was so far away from him and still so close.

—Over there, Virgil said, pointing with his whole body as if he had ferreted a rat from its hiding place.

Nina turned in that direction, expecting—what was she expecting? She had no idea. Perhaps—a sentence, a sentence that would sum up everything that needed to be said.

What she saw was not a sentence, not a brilliant fire burning words onto the black screen of outer space.

—Do you see? Virgil asked.

She did. She saw, and what she saw was good and beautiful and true, but it was too late to tell anyone.

Kelly Cherry has previously published twenty-one books (novels, stories, poetry, memoir, criticism, and reviews), nine chapbooks, and two translations of classical drama. Her newest full-length collection of poems, *The Life and Death of Poetry*, was published by Louisiana State University Press in 2013 and her newest chapbook, a group of poems titled *Vectors*, appeared from Parallel Press in December 2012. She was the first recipient of the Hanes Poetry Prize given by the Fellowship of Southern Writers for a body of work. Other awards include fellowships from the National Endowment for the Arts and the Rockefeller Foundation, the Bradley Major Achievement (Lifetime) Award, a USIS Speaker Award (the Philippines), a Distinguished Alumnus Award, three Wisconsin Arts Board fellowships, two WAB New Work awards, the Dictionary of Literary Biography Yearbook Award for Distinguished Book of Stories in 1999 (2000), and selection as a Wisconsin Notable Author. Her stories have appeared in *Best American Short Stories*, *The O. Henry Awards: Stories*, *The Pushcart Prize*, and *New Stories from the South*. In 2010, she was a Director's Visitor at the Institute for Advanced Study in Princeton. In 2012, she received both the Taramuto Prize for a story and the Carole Weinstein Prize for Poetry. In 2013, she received the L. E. Phillabaum Award for Poetry. Former Poet Laureate of Virginia and currently a member of the Electorate for Poets Corner at the Cathedral of St. John the Divine in New York, she is Eudora Welty Professor Emerita of English and Evjue-Bascom Professor Emerita in the Humanities at the University of Wisconsin–Madison. She and her husband live in Virginia. Further details appear on her Wikipedia page.